GUNMAN AT LARGE

In the height of its summer season
Whitsea is suffering from an outbreak
of robberies; Chief Inspector 'Jack'
Spratt wonders whether more than
one gang is involved. Sergeant Dick
Garrett gets into the act when a
gunman cuts loose on a caravan site,
and when masked men hold up the
Palladium box office. A snout, who
tries to play both sides against the
middle, makes complications which
are heightened by a murder before
Spratt can clear the Whitsea files.

Books by George Douglas
in the Linford Mystery Library:

UNHOLY TERROR
DOUBLE-CROSS
DEAD RECKONING
DEATH IN RETREAT
DEAD ON DELIVERY
LUCKLESS LADY
MURDER UNMOURNED
DEAD ON THE DOT
DEATH IN DUPLICATE
FINAL SCORE
END OF THE LINE
ONE TO JUMP
DEATH IN DARKNESS
UNWANTED WITNESS
ODD WOMAN OUT
CRIME MOST FOUL

GEORGE DOUGLAS

GUNMAN AT LARGE

Complete and Unabridged

LINFORD
Leicester

First published in Great Britain by
Robert Hale Limited
London

First Linford Edition
published 2006
by arrangement with
Robert Hale Limited
London

British Library CIP Data

Douglas, George
    Gunman at large.—Large print ed.—
Linford mystery library
    1. Detective and mystery stories
    2. Large type books
    I. Title
    823.9'14 [F]

    ISBN 1–84617–454–6

Published by
F. A. Thorpe (Publishing)
Anstey, Leicestershire

Set by Words & Graphics Ltd.
Anstey, Leicestershire
Printed and bound in Great Britain by
T. J. International Ltd., Padstow, Cornwall

This book is printed on acid-free paper

1

Police Constable Hayburn fitted the patrol car telephone into its recess.

'Shooting incident at the corporation caravan site, eh?' he grunted. 'It'll make a change, anyway.'

Scarr, his mate, nodded as he reversed the car and slid into the traffic, by no means heavy at four o'clock on a fine Saturday afternoon in August, which was headed towards the popular and thriving east coast resort of Whitsea. The two constables had almost reached the limit of their patrol beat when the call from Central had come. Now, open fields gave place first to scattered villas, then to rows of semis, to a parade of shops, to a newly-built council housing estate.

Four minutes later they swung into the entrance of what had once been a broad pasture between the coast road and the cliffs, but which now sprouted a heavy crop of touring caravans with their attendant cars drawn up alongside. An asphalted road ran through the centre of the site, a wooden building, immediately beyond the entrance, was lettered 'Site Warden,' and, placed discreetly in a corner, was a commodious range of toilets.

Scarr and Hayburn got out of their car, two alert and efficient young men whose first glance took in the small crowd of campers milling around a cream-coloured caravan. A tall, black-bearded man in khaki shirt and shorts broke away from them, waving exasperated arms, and came striding quickly towards the police officers.

'I'm Grinstead, site warden here. Man's been shot yonder. Not seriously, but I've sent for an ambulance. Seems the fellow who did it got away.'

'Right.' Hayburn, as the senior man, took over. 'We'll have a look.' He turned to Scarr as they went towards the caravan in Grinstead's wake. 'I'll leave you to deal with that mob, Mike. Get them away from there, listen to any of 'em who know anything, and tell the rest to scarper

2

— quick.' He lengthened his stride to catch up with the warden. 'And what do you know about this business, sir?'

'Very little, I'm afraid. I was working in my office when a woman dashed in to say her husband had been shot. I recognised her as a Mrs. Kendall of the Sprite Musketeer van here. The Kendalls booked in earlier this afternoon. They had made a reservation, of course. I went back with her and found the husband half-lying on one of the bunk beds. He was bleeding from a neck wound, but he seemed more shocked than damaged. I padded a towel and told the woman to press it to the wound, then ran across to the telephone in my office. Oh, I had asked Kendall what had happened and he gasped out something about an intruder who had pulled a gun on him, so I thought it best to call the police as well as the ambulance. There was no sign of any such intruder when I reached the van, nor on my way to the phone. Of course, with all these vehicles around he could have dropped out of sight at once.' He halted at the door of the Sprite. 'Look, it'll be a bit of a crush inside with two of us besides the Kendalls, and the ambulance men'll be here soon.'

'You're right, sir. How about if you give my mate a hand, see if you can find anybody who saw this marksman? I'll see you again later.'

Hayburn gave a perfunctory knock on the caravan door, announced 'Police,' and edged himself inside. There were two men and a woman in the caravan. One of the men, reclining on a bunk, was young, fair-haired, with sharp features and a long nose. His face was white and he held a bloodstained pad to the left side of his neck. The other man, a few years older, was short, slim and dark, with a narrow face and outstanding ears. The woman, not yet thirty, Hayburn judged, was also dark-haired, a brunette beauty with a rose and ivory complexion and a generous, perfectly-moulded mouth.

Hayburn addressed the wounded man. 'Now, sir, how's it going? We'll have you in the ambulance in a minute or two, but if you could answer a few questions first I'd appreciate it.'

'Oh, there's nothing much wrong with me,' the fair-haired man replied irritably. 'Just a superficial wound. No need to fuss with hospitals, really, but my wife insists on it.' He glanced at the brunette, frowning. Hayburn took out his notebook. 'If you could just give me the facts, sir . . . '

'We were travelling here from Deniston this afternoon. We pulled up in Pickering, went into a snack bar for a cup of tea. Got talking to a fellow there, very pleasant sort he seemed. Said he was in a bit of a jam, he'd come from Leeds by bus, having arranged to meet a friend with a car at Pickering and go on to Whitsea with him, but the friend hadn't turned up. He'd been hanging about for nearly two hours, but he said he thought he'd better get to Whitsea by the local bus and try and sort things out there.' He made a grimace of pain. 'You carry on, Dulcie. Talking's not so easy.'

'We offered him a lift,' the woman said, in a deep, husky contralto, 'and he seemed very grateful. We put him down outside the site here, checked in, and then

I went off to the shops across the road. When I got back I found Ivor collapsed and bleeding. This gentleman — ' she indicated the second man — 'was with him. I ran across to find the site warden at once.'

Hayburn, turning to the other man, saw, through the window, the flashing blue light of an ambulance entering the site. He said, 'Well, sir?'

'I'm Dennis Read,' the dark-haired man responded. 'I'm here with my wife and little boy, in the next van yonder. I heard a report and breaking glass, so I ran outside to see what had happened.' He pointed to the rear window. Hayburn had already noticed the starred glass with the neat hole in the middle. 'I did what I could for Mr. — er — here.'

'Our name's Kendall,' the woman said. 'And I'm sure we're very grateful, Mr. Read.'

'Just one other thing,' Hayburn said. 'We haven't had the rest of the story. You dropped this man outside the gate, then what?' His glance went from Kendall to his wife and back again. The man roused himself with an effort.

'My wife had gone shopping, I was in here unpacking. This man we'd just given a lift to pushed his way into the caravan and demanded money. I told him to clear out, he pulled out a gun and said I'd better unbelt or else. I wasn't having that. I rushed him, he fired. And then he disappeared. That's all I know.'

'Right, sir. The ambulance is here, so you and I, Mr. Read, will move out and make some room. You're going to the hospital with your husband, Mrs. Kendall?'

'You bet I am!'

'Then if you'd just step outside while they're looking after your husband, you can give me a description of this gunman.'

Five minutes later Hayburn and Scarr were in the site warden's office. 'Any luck?' Grinstead asked.

'We've got a good description from Mrs. Kendall,' Hayburn replied. 'Man in his late forties, tall loose-limbed, gangling sort of chap. Wide mouth, bad teeth, brown-haired. No hat, checked sports coat and dark grey trousers. Suede shoes.'

'I've phoned all that back to H.Q.,' Scarr said. 'But neither Mr. Grinstead here nor myself has found anybody on the site who saw him either coming or going. I suppose we'll have to make a search for the bullet, somewhere behind the caravan?'

'We'll wait till we get some help sent along,' Hayburn decided. 'Should have been here by now, anyway.'

'One point,' Grinstead said. 'What about his luggage?'

Hayburn grinned. 'I thought of that. If his tale was true, that he was travelling on holiday from Leeds to Whitsea, you'd naturally expect at least one suitcase. But Mrs. Kendall says he told them, when they picked him up at Pickering, that his friend with the car was transporting his stuff. Makes no sense to me. If the friend could take his luggage, why couldn't he have taken the man himself? The Kendalls didn't think to ask him that. Well, we'll have to find him. Can't have a man like that running around loose.'

Grinstead called, 'Come in,' as a knock

sounded on the office door. The door was pushed open by a lad in his early teens, in a khaki drill shirt, shorts and sandals. Intelligent blue eyes in a tanned face went to each of the three men in turn as the boy stood hesitating on the threshold.

'Now, then, young man,' the warden greeted. 'Colin, isn't it? What can we do for you?'

'Colin Taylor, Mr. Grinstead. We're down at the far end of the site, you know. It's just that I've heard about this shooting business. Is it true that a man is supposed to have walked on to the site and shot the owner of that Sprite? I mean, that's what people are saying.'

'Yes, it's true,' Grinstead said, and smiled at him. 'So what?'

'Well, I've been sitting in the snack bar across the road for the past hour, and I've been watching the cars and people coming in and out of here. And I didn't see anybody like this man with the gun.'

'He could have slipped in when you were looking the other way, or fetching yourself another coke or whatever.'

Hayburn said. 'In fact, that's what probably happened. Anyway, thanks for letting us know.' He made a gesture of dismissal, but young Colin Taylor stood his ground.

'No, honestly, I never took my eyes off the place. I mean, I'm interested in cars and caravans, and there were lots of them arriving. For instance. I saw the Sprite belonging to the man who was shot come in, towed by a Cortina. And it was only just after they'd arrived, wasn't it, that — '

'You'd see the outfit stop, then, to let the man they were giving a lift to get out of the car?' Hayburn asked sharply.

'They didn't stop. They came right down the road and turned straight in.'

'Did they now? You're sure of that?' He hardly waited for Colin's definitely-given assertion; through the open door he saw another police car draw up on the site. 'Come on,' he said to Scarr, 'here's the brains department arriving.'

★   ★   ★

Sergeant Richard Garrett, of the North Central Regional Crime Squad, which is based in Deniston, walked slowly, with an almost imperceptible limp, up from the beach towards his boarding house. He was extremely fed-up with Whitsea, with matters in general. An idle existence wasn't in his line at all.

He had recently, in the course of his professional duties, tangled with a man armed with an axe, who had inflicted grievous bodily harm on two members of his family. Before Garrett succeeded in disarming his man, he had received the edge of the axe deeply into his thigh. Blood transfusions had saved his life, the police doctor had ordered a month's convalescence. Three weeks of Whitsea, despite a spell of indifferent weather, had put the patient literally back on his feet. But the charms of the seaside had taken a beating. He wasn't allowed to swim, he had seen all the shows and he was no fisherman. Time was hanging very heavily upon his hands.

He therefore noted, with keen interest, the gathering of local police, and the general air of something-up, as he was passing the caravan site on his way to afternoon tea he could well do without. He didn't hesitate to walk on to the site, announce his profession to the nearest policeman and ask to be told what was happening.

The policeman, relegated to general keep-the-mob-away duties, gave him the facts. 'There's a bunch of the lads looking for the bullet,' he said. 'I reckon they've as much chance of finding it as I have of being made up to chief constable.' He stiffened to salute a youngish man, formally dressed in a dark blue suit, who had got out of a car which had drawn up alongside.

'Inspector Dykes, C.I.D.,' he muttered sideways to Garrett.

Dykes was a wide-shouldered, compactly-built man with a powdering of grey at his temples and steady brown eyes in a mobile, pleasant face. He looked Garrett up and down with an air of casual inquiry.

Garrett introduced himself once more and Dykes grinned.

'Ah! You're one of the delegation here, eh, sergeant?'

'Delegation, sir? I'm here on sick leave, and, incidentally, I'm sick of leave.' He returned Dykes' grin.

'Then you don't know that Chief Superintendent Hallam and Inspector Spratt of your set-up are here in Whitsea? We've had quite an outbreak of robberies — big stores and hotels mainly — and our Chief decided we could do with you experts to clear 'em up. Anyway, if you're at a loose end, you feel free to tag along here. I've just come from the hospital. Kendall, the shot man, isn't badly hurt but they're keeping him there overnight. I want another word with his wife, who's back here now. It's a crazy business, this shooting, and I hope we pick up the man responsible. Can't do much more till that happens.'

Garrett followed him to the Kendalls' caravan, where they found a small, slightly-built young woman, with fair hair and a bustling, efficient manner, administering a cup of tea to Mrs. Kendall.

'I'm Barbara Read,' she told Dykes. 'My husband and I, and our little boy, are in the van next to this one.'

'Yes. It was your husband who found Mr. Kendall shot, I believe, Mrs. Read. You didn't see the intruder yourself?'

'Oh, no, I was busy unpacking. We'd only arrived less than half an hour beforehand. There's lots to do when you get to a site and start settling in, you know.'

'Quite. And you're from — ?'

'Leicester.' She turned quickly to the other woman who was sitting quietly in a corner by the broken window. 'Drink up, Dulcie, there's another in the pot.'

'You two know each other quite well, then?' Dykes asked. 'I mean, you didn't meet for the first time today?'

Little Mrs. Read swung round to him again. 'What makes you think that? Oh, yes — because I called her Dulcie, eh? Well, let me tell you we caravanners don't go for any of this standoffishness. We get pally at once, 'specially when we're next door to each other.'

'You can't beat it,' Dykes returned

pleasantly. 'Now, Mrs. Kendall, I'm glad your husband's injury isn't a serious one and that he'll be with you again tomorrow. A bad start to your holiday but I trust the rest of it will compensate. How long are you staying, by the way?'

'We're here for a fortnight.'

'Like us,' Mrs. Read put in. 'And I'm glad we've got put next door to each other, dear. Nice neighbours on a site make your holiday, I always say.'

'I'm sure they do,' Dykes said. 'Mrs. Kendall, I have your husband's story of the incident, and yours too, of course. But now you've had time to think it over, is there anything else you can tell me about this man who attacked your husband?'

Mrs. Kendall put her cup down and looked thoughtfully at the caravan sky-light.

'No, I don't think so. We — that is, Ivor, my husband — got talking to him in the caff at Pickering, but then, Ivor's like that. A right sociable type, you know. Talk to anybody, he will.'

'Is Mr. Kendall apt to be careless about flashing his money wallet around? I'm wondering, you see, if he changed a note in the cafe and this man saw his wallet was well loaded, which I suppose it was?'

Mrs. Kendall's large brown eyes met Dykes' inquiring gaze.

'He did change a note there,' she said. 'I remember that.' She picked up a handbag from the seat beside her, snapped open and produced a bulging note-case. 'See, this is Ivor's. He gave it to me at the hospital, thought it'd be safer that way. So I suppose that fellow could have seen Ivor was carrying plenty.'

'Right,' Dykes said. 'Now things begin to make sense. You dropped the man outside the site here, he probably hung around, saw you go across to the shops and thought here was his chance to relieve your husband of that wad of notes. May I see the money a moment?'

He took the note-case the woman handed to him and flicked through its contents. He gave a soft whistle of surprise. 'Must be getting on for a hundred here. Does he usually carry so much around with him, even on holiday?'

'Oh, well,' Mrs. Kendall said defensively, 'you never know, what with the caravan and the car . . . And we do reckon to go it a bit when we're having our holidays, you know, shows and that, and a few meals in posh places.'

'Of course.' Dykes returned the notecase. 'Now, just one other thing. Did you notice anything unusual about this man you gave a lift to, apart from the description we've already got? I mean, for instance, his speech — had he an accent?'

She shook her head. 'He just talked like us.'

'You come from Deniston, I believe? You mean, then, he could also have been a Deniston man?'

'I suppose so, though he did say he came from Leeds.'

'That might help. Well, we've got to try to find the man. And I hope we won't have to bother you any more.' Dykes turned his head towards Garrett, still standing in the doorway. 'Anything special strike you, sergeant?'

'I don't think so, sir. I — ' Garrett seemed about to add something and then to think better of it. He eased himself down the caravan steps and walked back with Dykes towards the warden's office.

'Thanks, sir,' he said. 'I was absolutely at a loose end, and you have helped to pass a bit of time for me.'

'That's all right, sergeant. You're staying near here?'

'At Cliffside. It's a boarding house just up the road. I'll keep a general look-out, in case this gunman returns to the scene of the crime, shall I?'

Dykes chuckled. 'We're hoping to grab him before long. I've got house-to-house enquiries started and they should turn something up. Also, he may try to find a bed somewhere in the town, so we'll warn as many people who let accommodation as we can. It's a big job, but we've done it before. And, by the way, I'm due at a conference with your people this evening. Any messages I can pass on?'

'Give 'em my kindest regards, sir, and say I'll be back on the job soon. As a matter of fact, the sooner the better. I'm no glutton, for work, but hanging about is fair ridiculous.'

2

Garrett was practically a son of the house at Cliffside. He had accompanied his parents there for a seaside holiday year after year throughout his boyhood. The Whites, who ran the place, were now middle-aged. Mrs. White had fussed over the convalescent as if she had been his own mother.

There was some excitement in the Cliffside dining room that evening. The police had visited the house, asking questions, the affair, practically on the boarding house doorstep, was reported at length in the local evening paper. Like most policemen on holiday, Garrett never advertised his profession, and Mr. and Mrs. White respected his wishes in the matter. He sat and listened to the boarding house knowall propounding, to an uninterested audience, just how the police should act in such a case. Mr. White, who served at table while his wife did the cooking, caught Garrett's eye and winked unobtrusively as he brought in the sweet course.

'Going out tonight, Dick?' Mrs. White asked him when, following a routine which had become custom, he had gone into the kitchen to give a hand with the washing up.

'Only for a walk — shan't be late in.'

He slipped a plastic mac into the pocket of his jacket, for the evening, after a breezy, bright day, had become overcast. He approached the caravan site and, on an impulse, turned into it. There was an atmosphere of relaxation about the place now. A few groups of children were playing quietly, two men, absorbed in a mechanical world, had their heads inside the bonnet of a car, a woman shook out a pair of beach towels and pegged them to a small washing line.

Garrett walked along the main roadway of the site, giving a quick, casual-seeming glance as he passed the two caravans belonging to the Kendall and Read families. Curtains were drawn in the latter; he remembered Mrs. Read had mentioned they had a child, now, no doubt, put to bed. He caught a glimpse of three adults in the Kendalls' van, recognising Mrs. Read and a man who, he guessed, was her husband. All of them were talking eagerly.

And why shouldn't they? Garrett wondered if his police-trained mind was making too much of a circumstance which probably had an explanation so simple that, on the point of mentioning it in Dykes' presence earlier, he had pulled himself up, not wishing to appear foolish.

According to the women's stories, the Reads were from Leicester, the Kendalls from Deniston, Garrett's own West Riding city. Yet Kendall's Cortina, and Read's Triumph Herald, both had Deniston registration letters. The Herald was new, with a very recently-issued number. It could, of course, have been bought from a Deniston agent, even though Read didn't live in that city. It was one of those points which, insignificant though they may prove to be, nag at the mind of an investigating officer until he has settled the matter, one way or another, to his own satisfaction.

Garrett strolled to the far end of the site where, beyond a stout cliff-top guard rail, Whitsea Bay spread out below him. It was getting rapidly dark, and the bay's necklace of promenade lights twinkled brightly up at him. He turned, and angled across the grass between the nearest caravans until he was walking back, parallel to the site roadway, behind the second row of vehicles which faced on to it. Curiosity, heightened by boredom, had suggested a spot of eavesdropping by the Kendalls' caravan.

But as it came into his view he stopped quickly, moving into the shadow of a van whose occupants, to judge from its closed-up, unlighted appearance, and the fact that no car stood alongside, were having a night out on the town. Somebody else besides himself, it seemed, was interested in the Kendalls' caravan. By the light of one of the lamps in the roadway beyond the site, Garrett had caught a glimpse of a figure lurking beneath the van's windows, which were now curtained.

A slim figure of medium height. Could be a youth, or a woman in shorts and sweater. But not there for any legitimate purpose, that was for sure.

The caravan door was opened suddenly, letting out a flood of light. The curvaceous form of Mrs. Kendall appeared on the threshold. And at once the listener dodged away, behind the van and out of sight. Mrs. Kendall emptied a teapot into a waste bin, went back up the van steps, closed the door.

Garrett walked forward. There was no sign of the dodger now. Probably scared, had decided to give up whatever it was he or she had been doing. Garrett circled the van, and those in the immediate vicinity. There was nobody about at all. He stepped quietly back to the Kendalls' caravan. Mrs. Read's voice came clearly to him from inside it, and he saw that one of the curtained windows was set slightly open.

'And supposing he does get caught, what then?'

A man's voice answered her. 'Not to worry love. He got clear, they won't put the finger on him now.' That was Read speaking, Garrett guessed.

'Which is all very well, Dennis,' Mrs. Kendall replied, 'but where does it leave us?'

'That's for Molly to decide. I'll get in touch first thing in the morning.' Garrett heard the rattle of a cup in its saucer. 'Look, if I'm going to do this thing I'd better get operating. Shan't be long, with luck.'

Mrs. Read said, with more than a touch of doubt in her voice, 'Well, I suppose it can't do any harm.'

There was a movement inside the caravan and Garrett walked swiftly away, towards the site roadway. A glance over his shoulder showed him Read coming out of the Kendalls' caravan. The man was looking down at something he held in his hand, something which he then pushed into a jacket pocket. Garrett went across the grass to the nearby toilets. The men's section was empty, he stood in the doorway, watching.

Read turned along the roadway, moving quickly away from the entrance

24

towards the far end of the site, from which Garrett himself had just come. Garrett shrugged, watching him. He had no good reason for following the man, furthermore, his injured leg was beginning to tell him he had used it enough for one day. The sooner he was resting it in front of the T.V. screen at Cliffside, the better.

The slim figure he had seen listening in at the Kendalls' caravan appeared from behind a parked car some distance away, between Garrett and Read. The policeman now saw it was a lad in his early teens and it was obvious he was shadowing Read. He was walking swiftly and silently over the grass and there was that tense wariness about his movements which Garrett himself had experienced so often when he had been on a trailing job.

Garrett simply had to join in. He couldn't leave it there, damaged leg or no. He must find out, if possible, where those two were headed. He would, at any rate, go as far as the site boundary where the railings were. He cut across the grass, working his way through the assemblage of vans, most of the occupants of which were beginning to settle down for the night.

He reached the railings, but could see nothing of either Read or his follower. This was the end of the site and, oddly enough, it seemed much better lighted now than when he had visited it a few moments previously. He saw the answer at once. In a corner, to his left, the fence turned back to enclose one of the lateral boundaries of the site and in the angle was a wooden gate, near which a concrete lamp-post supported a sodium light which had just been switched on. He crossed to the gate. From it, obviously serving the site, a steep asphalted path, with a tubular iron handrail alongside, led down to the beach.

Garrett went through the gate. Below him, clearly visible in the promenade lights, Read was moving almost at a run. And, at a safe distance behind him, but keeping station, was the youth.

That was that, then, Garrett reflected. He wasn't going any further. The thought of dogging after them to the promenade, with the steep slope to climb again afterwards was asking a bit too much. He'd just go a little way to see in what direction Read turned when he reached sea-level, and then pack it up for the night. He stopped at a convenient vantage point and watched the man from the caravan, the man from Leicester who drove a Triumph Herald with a Deniston registration. He watched too, the teenager who seemed so extremely interested in Read.

When he reached the promenade, busy with evening strollers, Read turned to his left, away from the town and the pier. Near this point the promenade came to an end, where a stream cut down between the cliffs to form a narrow, bush-clad ravine. Beyond the promenade a narrow concrete bridge spanned the stream, giving access to a rough path which wound up the side of the far cliff encircling Whitsea Bay at its northern end. It was a path much frequented by enthusiastic walkers during the day and by lovers when darkness had fallen. Read crossed the bridge and began to climb the cliff path. Behind him, the lad followed warily.

Garrett was completely puzzled now. Read, he was certain, was not headed for any tender assignation, yet the cliff path led only to Clinton, some five miles away. If Read had business at that small fishing village he would surely have gone by car, along the coast road. And why was the boy so interested in Read's movements? Garrett wished he knew the answers.

An idea struck him. It wouldn't be too hard going for him down the path to the promenade, and, a couple of hundred yards to his right was one of the cliff lifts which, for a modest sum of threepence, would put him back within easy distance of Cliffside in a few seconds. So he'd go down as far as the small bridge and wait there awhile, to see if those two or either of them came back. His watch said nine o'clock when he reached the bridge and sat down on a wooden seat which faced it. He would keep watch for half an hour, no longer.

Few people were at this end of the promenade now. There was little to occupy his attention, darkness was approaching quickly and Garrett soon found time beginning to drag. Twenty minutes rest took the ache out of his leg, he looked up at the empty cliff path and decided to follow it — just for five minutes and then back again.

Wooden steps had been set at intervals to ease the steepest pitches, close-growing bushes of gorse and bramble lined the way with patches of rough grass between them. Garrett met a couple descending, hand in hand, then a woman with a dog, followed by two men, middle-aged, in holiday garb, discussing the local beer as they descended rapidly en route for an evening pint. That seemed to clear the cliff walk of people, for, when Garrett reached the limit he had set himself, there was nobody else in sight or hearing.

Then, as he turned to descend, there came a quick, snapping report somewhere to his left. It was followed at once by an indignant yell, and a half-stifled scream. What seemed to be a heavy body went crashing through the bushes downhill in the darkness, parallel to the path.

There was still light enough to see one's footing, and Garrett turned at once off the path, towards the seat of commotion. Behind a high gorse bush he found a man and a woman. The man's arms were about his companion, he seemed to be trying without much success to calm her, for she was sobbing hysterically and struggling to get away from him.

'What happened?' Garrett used his official voice. The man, who was short and plump, somewhere in his middle forties, peered at him.

'Some damn fool — one of these Peeping Toms, I guess — took a pot shot at us. Would you credit that?' He gave the woman a sharp admonitory shake. 'For Pete's sake, Dora, shut up! It's all over, the fellow's gone, there's nothing to make a fuss about.'

'I heard the shot,' Garrett said. 'He didn't hit either of you?'

'No. Though he wasn't far off. I heard the bullet sing past my ear like an angry hornet. Reminded me of the old days, it did. The war, I mean. I saw a lot of action.'

'Can you describe this fellow?'

The man shook his head. 'His face was just a sort of blur, he seemed to appear, sudden like, over the top of the gorse bush there, I saw him lift his hand and push something forward. Then there was the shot, and he ran off. Didn't you see him?'

'I didn't,' Garrett replied. 'He went down through the bushes. Are you two staying in Whitsea?'

He was aware at once of a sudden tension in the couple.

'Er — what's it matter where we come from?' The man laughed shortly. 'Anyway, it's getting late, time we were thinking of home. I'll say goodnight, mate.'

Garrett ignored the hint. 'You'll report this incident to the police, of course?'

'Police? What the heck for?' Garrett saw how the woman shrank back as the man answered. 'No harm's been done, just a nut-case having his bit of fun. We aren't bothering about the police, and that's flat.'

'Haven't you read in the evening paper about the shooting incident at the caravan site today? This could be the same man, you know, and in any case, you can't have people running around taking pot shots just when they feel like it.'

The man pushed himself forward and fronted Garrett angrily.

'Look here chum. I haven't seen an evening paper, I don't give a damn who gets shot as long as it isn't me. We're not going to the police, and if you want to know why, let me tell you my friend and me don't want it known we're out together tonight.' He ignored a gasp of consternation from his companion. 'Is that straight enough for you? Now you push off, like a good boy, and leave us to mind our own business.'

Garrett's leg was beginning to ache again. He had had enough of argument.

'I must insist you report this affair,' he said sharply. 'I'm a police officer and it's my duty to see that you do yours.'

'A policeman!' The woman gasped, and shrank farther back into the darkness, but her companion's reply was an outraged snort.

'And how do we know you're a copper?'

Garrett's hand went to his breast pocket. 'I've my warrant card here. If you'll accompany me to the nearest lamp, you can read it.'

The man was silent for a few moments. When he spoke it was in a more reasonable tone.

'Look pal, I can see your point. If there is a chap roaming around with a loaded gun, you'll want to get your hands on him. But we can't help you there. The fellow's gone, we've told you what happened. We don't want to go to a police station where we'll have to give our names and so on. We've broken no law, being here together, but it would land us into trouble if the fact got out. Surely you'll appreciate that? We've told you the story, you're a policeman. That's enough, isn't it?'

'The snag is,' Garrett returned, 'that I'm not on the local force — I'm just here on holiday. The Whitsea C.I.D'll need a first-hand report from you, not a sort of hearsay tale from me.'

'I see . . . It's a pity you didn't chase that chap when he bolted off from here. He must have passed very close to you. I'd have thought, being a policeman . . . '

Garrett laughed shortly. 'I happen to have a gammy leg just now. That's why.'

'I see,' the other repeated. He turned to the woman and squeezed her hand reassuringly. 'Look, love, we've got to do what our friend here says. But it'll be all right, I promise you.'

'No!' Her voice sounded hysterical again. 'I'm not going to any police station — I don't care what he says!'

'Tell you what,' Garrett suggested, 'I'll come with you. I'll explain to the officer in charge that you don't want anything in the way of publicity. I can promise you your wishes will be respected. That's fair enough, isn't it?'

'Sure it is.' The man spoke quite heartily. 'Come on, love, and let's get it over. It's late enough as it is, and by the time you land back home — Well, we've no more of that time to waste, have we?'

He took her arm and, moving past Garrett, led her on to the cliff path. Garrett followed them. There was light enough from the promenade lamps below to see the path clearly, and just room enough for two people to walk abreast. The couple began to descend at a rapid rate. Garrett strove to keep up with them, but he lost ground at every step.

'Sorry,' he called out, 'but I can't go at your pace.'

The man glanced over his shoulder. 'See you at the bottom, eh?' He nudged the woman and they began to go forward at a run.

Garrett pulled up, cursing silently. Subconsciously, he had anticipated trickery while knowing there was little he could do about it if it took place. There would be no waiting at the bottom for those two. Already they were almost out of sight.

He plodded on downwards. Just beyond the bridge, adjacent to the end of the promenade, was a small car park from which a narrow, steep road ran up the side of the ravine to the main road above.

He saw the couple cross the bridge, walking quickly now. The man looked back and gave a brief wave of triumph at the solitary figure struggling downwards. Then he and the woman darted across to the car park, there came the sound of a revved-up engine, headlamps beamed on as the car swung off up the narrow road and disappeared.

3

The cliff lift gave a slight shudder, a gentle bump, and began to ascend. Garrett, who had been the last passenger to enter the small cabin — nobbut just in time for this trip, as the attendant had remarked — looked around at his fellow passengers. Two elderly couples, a man and a woman with a fractious, over-tired child, and, in one corner, a teenage lad in shorts upon whom Garrett's glance became fixed. He couldn't be sure, but he would have chanced a bet that it was the same youth he had seen on the caravan site, the youth who had followed Read down to the end of the promenade and across the bridge to the cliff path.

Garrett's tiredness, his longing to get back to his lodgings and put his feet up, faded quickly. He knew, for his own satisfaction, that he must try to have a word with this boy. When the lift came to rest at the cliff top, Garrett, in last, was out first. He waited by the gates which gave on to a wide esplanade, lined at one side with big hotels and the more expensive type of boarding house.

The lad came bustling out, looking at his wrist watch. It was almost ten o'clock and quite dark now away from the lighted streets. Naturally, he would be in a hurry to get back to his temporary home, Garrett realised; perhaps, after all, it wasn't fair to delay him now. As Garrett hesitated over this thought, the boy looked up and his step faltered. There was no consternation in his expression, however, as his eyes took in the tall, pleasant-faced young man who stood almost in his way. Suddenly, he grinned.

'Good evening. I've seen you before, haven't I? On the caravan site just off Northway Road?'

'I was there this afternoon,' Garrett returned. He didn't think the lad could have spotted him on his second visit that evening.

'Yes. You were with the plainclothes man who seemed to be in charge, sort of. You went with him into the van where the man had been shot. Are you a policeman, too?'

'As it happens, yes.' Garrett liked the look of this youth. His dark brown hair was cut sensibly short, he had an open, ingenuous face and alert eyes. 'Though I'm not a member of the local force. I was just there by courtesy of Detective Inspector Dykes.'

'But you are a policeman.' He sounded impulsively eager. 'Look, I wonder if . . . You see, there's something . . . '

'We'd better walk on,' Garrett said. 'I take it you're staying at the site?' The boy nodded. 'Right. I'm going that way myself. And your parents may be getting a little worried on your account, you know. It is rather late.'

The lad gave a derisive snort. 'They won't bother. They're here to play golf chiefly, all and every day. And then, at nights, they meet up with some friends at the Royal Arms and stay there till kicking-out time. I'm on my own most of the day, but then, a seaside holiday is so ideal for a youngster, isn't it? So much to do, so many friends to make! What a load of old cods' wallop!'

The bitter sarcasm in his voice held more than a touch of self-pity, Garrett thought.

'Ah, well,' he said, 'you know the saying, lad — into every life some rain must fall. My name's Dick Garrett. What's yours?'

'Colin Taylor. We're from Deniston. Came last week, and we're here till next Saturday. Look, Mr. Garrett, about that shooting business. The fellow who did it was supposed to have walked into the site and up to the Kendalls' caravan. Well, he didn't — walk in, I mean. I was in the snack bar opposite the site and I'd have seen him if he had done. So he was either on the site already or he came in by the back gate, the one which leads down to the prom. Actually, I doubt if he did — come in by the back gate, I mean. I know another fellow on the site — his name's Keith Jackson, he's thirteen, a year younger than I am — and their Holivan Ten is berthed right alongside that small gate. And I asked him and he didn't see the man come in and he was sitting outside — his people had asked some other campers to a picnic tea — all the time, facing the gate, actually.'

As they had walked along towards the end of the esplanade the words had poured eagerly from Colin Taylor's lips, but Garrett was listening with some caution. Was this just a case of a bored teenager, his interest aroused by the arrival of the police, making up a story on very slim evidence? Garrett had met the same thing before in his job, and not only once, either.

'You know, Colin,' he said, 'you should have told the police about this when they were on the site.'

'But I did! I went to the warden's office and there was one of the patrolmen there and I told him — well, at least, about not seeing the man go into the site — but he didn't seem to think I knew what I was talking about, and then the inspector arrived and nobody had any more time for me.'

'So,' Garrett said slowly, 'later on you thought you'd do a spot of sleuthing on your own, eh? You listened outside the Kendalls' van.'

'I — I — ' Young Taylor was totally confused now. 'How did you — ? I didn't mean any harm, honestly.' He turned to look at Garrett, a thoughtful frown on his brow. 'You mean, you saw me? Were you doing a spot of snooping yourself, Mr. Garrett?'

There was no impertinence in the question. Garrett chuckled.

'Policemen don't snoop, you know. They carry out observation.'

Colin echoed the chuckle. 'Even when they're on holiday, and not a member of the local force?'

Bored teenager or not, this lad had none of his buttons missing.

'Sometimes a busman's holiday can be quite interesting, you know, Colin. So did you hear anything of importance?'

'Not a lot. There was Mrs. Kendall there and Mr. Read and his wife. They all sounded very friendly, quite like old pals, somehow. Mr. Read said it was a pity all this had happened but nothing could be done at the moment and that he'd have to let somebody know, but I didn't catch the name. And then, ever so suddenly, the van door opened and Mrs. Kendall came out. I thought she'd be bound to see me, and believe me, Mr. Garrett, I nearly passed out, I was so scared. But she didn't spot me and I thought I'd better scarper before somebody did — I wasn't looking for trouble. I went along the site to see if that chap Jackson I told you about was around. I was going to suggest a stroll. But they'd all gone out, so I went for one on my own.'

'Following Mr. Read down to the prom, across the little bridge and up the cliff path,' Garrett said drily.

'Oh, my gosh! Did you do the same — follow me, I mean?'

'I saw you from the path which leads down from the site. I was curious, you see. About both of you.'

Colin shrugged. 'I'd nothing to do,' he muttered, 'and it seemed it might be a bit of fun.'

'You thought he was up to something odd?'

'Well . . . No, not exactly. He seemed to be in a dickens of a hurry to get somewhere and when I saw him headed for the cliffs — well, there isn't anywhere to get to up there, I mean, not as late in the day as this.'

'So what happened?'

'Nothing, really. I couldn't stick too close to him, you know. There's a dip in the ground about half way up and I lost him there for a few moments. When I got to this dip, there was a seat and he was sitting on it, smoking a cigarette. I had to go on past him, of course. It would have looked odd to stop, or turn back. I went on for a little distance, then risked a look. It was getting pretty dark by that time but I could see the seat all right. It was empty. He'd gone. So I hurried back, expecting to spot him again, returning to the bridge. He wasn't anywhere in sight. So that was that. I carried on down to the prom and walked back along it as far as the pier, just for something to do. Then I turned round and treated myself to threepennyworth up the cliff. I say, Mr. Garrett, are you interested in Mr. Read, too?'

'I've no cause to be, Colin. If I were

you — Hullo, what's up here? More trouble?'

They had reached the end of the esplanade and had turned into Sewell Road, which ran in a gentle slope down to Northway. There were tennis courts and putting greens here at the corner, and, beyond them, the imposing façade of one of Whitsea's most popular variety theatres, the Palladium. Small groups of holiday-makers were to be found here at all hours of the day, examining the display glossies of the famous stars who were appearing at the Palladium for the summer season, reading the bills or forming a patient queue at the booking office. This was now closed for the day, and the small crowd of people milling around the entrance weren't interested, for once, in show business. They were gawping at the two police cars drawn up on the edge of the pavement, and taking only reluctant notice of the constable who, standing at the foot of the steps, was monotonously urging them to move on, please, there was nothing to be seen.

Colin Taylor darted across the road

before Garrett could restrain him. After a moment's hesitation, Garrett followed. He told himself he'd better advise the lad not to hang around and get in the way, that it was time, in any case, for him to be getting back to the caravan site. But he knew this was a mere self-excuse to indulge his own curiosity.

'Hullo, sarge! You got a nose for these jobs, or something?'

It was the constable he had seen and spoken to on the caravan site earlier that day. Garrett grinned.

'You still on duty? Doing a round-the-clock, like?'

'Two to ten this week, me. But this thing turned up, and you know how it is.' He broke off to assure a fussy, pushing woman she'd be able to read all about it in the morning paper. 'Some bright lads did the till here,' he went on quietly as Garrett moved to his side. 'Held up the box office woman just when she'd done cashing-up for the day. Go on in if you like, sarge. Inspector Dykes is there, he won't mind, I'm sure.'

'Right.' Colin Taylor had disappeared

and Garrett went up the steps into the foyer. From the theatre itself he could hear the voice of an internationally-famous comedian, punctuated by gales of laughter. The second house was drawing to its close.

Dykes was standing in front of a leatherette-covered bench on which a blowsy, fat woman was reclining in an exhausted-seeming sprawl. She had fluffed-out hair dyed a startling red, the heavy make-up she wore failed to conceal her age; her ear-rings, her jewel-laden fingers and her smart black and red blouse were incongruous contrast to her shapeless, shabby skirt and the soiled canvas shoes on her large feet. Garrett grinned briefly. Naturally, only the top half was important, the public wouldn't see the rest.

Beside her, holding a glass of water and fidgeting restlessly was a short plump man in dinner jacket and black tie whom Garrett recognised as the Palladium manager.

As the Deniston man came forward to join the group, Dykes turned his head.

'Ah, sergeant!' he said pleasantly. That was all, but, besides telling Garrett he was welcome enough there, Dykes had implied to the manager and his employee that Garrett's presence was official. They would accept it as such without further explanations.

'Now, Beryl.' Dykes turned back to the woman. 'It's all over, you didn't get hurt, you've had your bit of hysterics, so now you can answer a few questions.'

The woman sniffed and dabbed at her eyes with a scrap of handkerchief, then she heaved herself up into a sitting position and glared at the inspector.

'It's all very well for you to talk, Charlie Dykes,' she said acidly, 'but I'd like to know how you'd feel if a couple of thugs had threatened to shoot you dead with a revolver!'

'Right,' Dykes said patiently. 'So there were two of them. Both armed?'

'I only saw one gun. I mean, this fellow kept it pointed at me while t'other made me hand over the takings. I mean, what else could I do, Mr. Best? I mean, anybody 'ud have done the same.'

'Of course, Mrs. Graham.' The manager nodded. 'I'm not blaming you at all. Nobody's blaming you.'

Dykes broke in again. 'Let's have a description, Beryl.' He raised a finger to a man who had come out of the metal-grilled booking office just inside the foyer doors. 'And let's have it quick. The constable here will take it down and we'll get it relayed at once.'

Mrs. Graham put her hands to her scarlet hair. 'Well, y'see, it's a bit difficult. They was wearing these nylon masks made out of stockings. So you couldn't see their features, not more'n a blur, like. They was mediumish in height and both wore dark suits. The one as held the gun and told me to hand over spoke in a sorta hoarse whisper. That's all I can tell you.'

'Young men?'

'Youngish, both of 'em, as far as I could tell.'

Dykes said, 'Right. Get that off, Allenby, what there is of it. Nothing in the office, I suppose?'

Allenby shook his head as he went out. Dykes spoke to the woman again.

'That'll be all, then, Beryl. You'd better get yourself home.' He looked across at the manager. 'I'd like a word with you in private, sir.'

'Of course, inspector. My office.' He led the way to a door opposite and Dykes, following him, motioned to Garrett to go along too. At the door, Best halted, his head cocked sideways.

'Last turn just ending,' he said. 'They'll be coming out now. But they won't need me.' He showed them in to a tidy, efficient-looking place and gave them chairs. Tentatively, he offered cigarettes and drinks, both of which were refused. 'You're on duty, of course,' he said. 'Now, inspector . . . '

'You told me, I think, sir, that you were in the auditorium when this robbery took place?'

'That is so. It's my custom to go in before the interval and again after it, for — oh, five, perhaps ten minutes each time. I like to get the mood of the house, judge audience reaction to the various acts, you know.'

'So you left the foyer, where, in the box

office, Mrs. Graham was cashing-up for the day. And the thieves got away with quite a haul?'

Best grinned wryly. 'I'm afraid they did. Saturday night, you know. Like all seaside resorts, Whitsea has a big weekend turnover of visitors. And very many of them, when they arrive on Saturday, book for a show straightaway. It wouldn't take much intelligence, on the part of a thief, to work out that when the booking office closes on Saturday nights, there's quite a bit of money here. On my way home,' he added, 'I always put it into the bank's night deposit safe.'

'You employ a commissionaire, don't you? I've seen him around usually. Where's he now?'

'Not on duty tonight. He suffers from occasional bouts of asthma — a war legacy — and he had a severe attack about seven this evening. I sent him home in a taxi.'

'And later on you left Mrs. Graham on her own while you spent some time inside the theatre? I'm afraid your insurance company won't take a very bright view of that, sir.'

Best frowned. 'No, confound it! Yet how was I to know?' He broke off to indulge in some moments' deep worry. 'I just didn't think, I suppose,' he muttered. 'Didn't realise Lodge, the doorman, wouldn't be there as usual.'

'Now, about Mrs. Graham,' Dykes went on. 'She's been working here for several seasons, I believe?'

'This is her third. I say, inspector, you seem to know her quite well.'

'She's a native of Whitsea, as I am, sir. You're quite satisfied with her? In the position of trust she holds here?'

'I have no complaints at all. She is excellent in dealing with the customers, her accounts are kept perfectly and she never makes a mistake in booking. Her speech may be somewhat uneducated but she has a head for business, without a doubt.'

Dykes pushed his chair back and rose. 'That's about all we can do here tonight, sergeant,' he said to the silent Garrett, and then turned again to Best. 'You'll lock the place up as usual, of course, sir, and we'll see if we can catch these villains for you.'

While they had been talking, the Palladium had emptied, and when they came out to the foyer the lights were being extinguished, the place was closing for the night. Promising the manager to keep in touch, Dykes led the way outside. The constable with whom Garrett had spoken had been replaced by another man.

'All right, Edwards,' Dykes said to him, 'you can leave this now.' He wished the man goodnight and jerked a thumb at a car parked across the street.

'I'll run you home, sergeant. Cliffside, isn't it?'

Garrett accepted the offer with gratitude. He'd done more than enough on that leg today. Dykes swung the car away from the kerb.

'Well, and what do you think of our latest local crime?'

'I was interested in what you appeared to be thinking of it, sir. I got a distinct impression that a put-up job was in your mind.'

'It could be, you know. A couple of clients casing the job would find out Best's habit of leaving the foyer at intervals, easy enough. But normally the commissionaire would be handy and he'd represent quite an extra risk. And the job was done when Lodge had been taken ill and sent home. It does make you think.'

'I've known chaps who could fake an asthma attack, sir.'

'Yes . . . Trouble is, I'd stake my job on old Jim Lodge being one hundred per cent straight. Have to check it, though.'

'The cashier, sir? I thought you were a bit doubtful there.'

'I've known Beryl Graham most of my life. She's married to a small-time car dealer, at least, that's what he's supposed to be, a Londoner. He hasn't any form with us, but — well, he's the sort of chap you'd never be surprised to see up in a magistrates' court — on any charge you could think of. As soon as we arrived, by the way, Beryl insisted on being searched, said she wanted to be sure we didn't suspect her of stashing the money away. I had the women's room gone over with a fine toothcomb, also, of course.' His foot touched the car's brakes. 'Well, here's your humble abode, sergeant. Glad to have met you. See you again, maybe before you leave.'

'I hope so, sir, and many thanks.' Garrett got out of the car and Dykes, in a swift U-turn, headed back with a final friendly wave.

4

Garrett was late to breakfast the following morning. His overworked leg had ached intolerably when he had got to bed and the aspirin he took failed to act until long past midnight. But then he had fallen into a deep sleep and this morning he felt very much refreshed and quite free from pain. He despatched an excellent breakfast and wandered into the lounge, to be greeted by two of his fellow-guests, plump, bald Mr. Lawrence and his tall thin wife.

'Going to be a nice day, I think.' Mr. Lawrence peered over his reading glasses. He rustled the Sunday paper he was glancing at. 'I see there was quite a bit of excitement in Whitsea last night.'

'You mean the raid on the Palladium box office?'

'That's right. It's in the stop press. What with that, and these big robberies that have been going on, and that shooting business at the caravan site, I reckon the local police will have their hands full. Of course, if I had my way . . . '

Garrett listened for some ten minutes to Lawrence's theories on how to put a stop, once and for all, to crime. As he didn't know he was talking to a policeman, he caused Garrett a slight amusement which helped him to suffer the monotonous voice going on and on. But the time came when he had had enough of it, and he began to search for some means of escape. At this point fortune favoured him.

He had heard the front door bell ring and Mr. White going along the passage to answer it. He caught the murmur of voices. Then the proprietor of Cliffside put his head into the lounge.

'Someone to see you, Dick.'

Surprised, Garrett excused himself to the Lawrences and went out. 'I've taken him to your room,' Mr. White said.

'Thanks, pop.' In consideration of his injury, Garrett had been given a room on the ground floor. It was small, and not well-lighted, an apartment the Whites normally used only when they were compelled to squeeze an extra visitor in, but it was comfortably furnished and it suited Garrett admirably.

A tall, well-built man, who had been standing by the small window which looked on to the back garden, turned round at Garrett's entrance, grinning broadly.

'Now, young man, how's it going, then?'

'Mr. Spratt!' There was warmth and delight in Garrett's response. 'My, it's good to see you! Sit down, the chair's a bit small, but it's stout enough.' He perched himself on the edge of the bed. 'I met Inspector Dykes yesterday, I got sort of unofficially involved in that shooting job at the caravan site. He said you and Mr. Hallam were here.'

'It was Dykes who told me where you were staying,' Inspector 'Jack' Spratt, of the North Central Regional C.I.D., replied. 'So I thought I'd come and look you up. How's that leg behaving? I notice you're still limping a bit.'

'Oh, it's improving fast now, thanks.

Still inclined to play me up if I'm on it too long, but otherwise okay. I'm going back to Deniston next Saturday, and I hope the quack will pass me fit for duty. I'm fed up with doing nothing, sir.'

'We'd be pleased to have you back, that's certain, Dick,' Spratt replied, 'but it would be foolish to rush things. Mr. Hallam sent his regards and best wishes, by the way.'

'He's here with you, isn't he? Mr. Dykes told me they'd called us — you, I mean — in over these hotel and store robberies.'

'We came here yesterday,' Spratt said. 'Had a short conference with the local brass and then Mr. Hallam went back to Deniston. Meanwhile, I'm holding the baby here, and between ourselves it looks like being a very fractious sort of infant. I don't like these advisory-capacity jobs, working with another force. It's always best when we can get down to a job with our own lads, only, as you know, it doesn't always happen that way.' He put his head on one side and regarded Garrett speculatively. 'You really meant it when you said you were fed up with doing nothing, eh?'

Garrett sat forward eagerly. 'I sure did, Mr. Spratt.'

'Then if you haven't any plans for this morning, why not come along with me? I'm meeting the local C.I.D. officers at ten-thirty, for another pow-wow. To tell you the truth, Dick, I could do with a bit of moral support, and you might find it interesting.'

'I'd love it. You mean, you're running into a bit of local antagonism? 'We don't want any regional crime squad brought in, we can do the job ourselves' type of thing?'

'Something like that. Inspector Dykes is all right, but one or two of the others!' He shrugged. 'Still, the Whitsea Chief Constable asked for us, and that's that. But the sooner I get this job behind me, the better I'll be pleased.' He glanced at his watch. 'Well, if you're ready, we'll be getting along.'

Whitsea Central Police Station was newly-built, modern in design, well equipped. Spratt parked his car in one of the bays marked 'Visitors Only' and led the way to the main office. Here they were taken over by a civilian clerk who conducted them along a passage to a mezzanine floor, and finally, to a door lettered 'Superintendent Welling. C.I.D.' His knock brought a sharp, 'Come in, then!' and Spratt preceded Garrett into a bright, sunny room where three men were seated at one end of a large table. Garrett recognised Inspector Dykes, on the left of a burly man with iron-grey hair, a bulbous nose and a bushy moustache above a hard mouth and a rocklike chin. Opposite Dykes was a younger man, with reddish hair and heavy features running to fat.

'Ah, Spratt!' the burly man greeted. His voice was low, almost a growl. He glanced ostentatiously at a wall clock which showed two minutes after half-past ten. 'I was beginning to wonder where you'd got to. And who's this feller?'

'Detective Sergeant Garrett, sir,' Spratt said smoothly. 'A member of my staff in Deniston. You'll find him . . . '

'Why wasn't he here with you and

Hallam last night, then?'

'He wasn't available then, sir.' Garrett caught Dykes' eye and the inspector's lid flickered. It was clear Spratt didn't intend to go into detailed explanations regarding Garrett's presence, and it was also clear that Dykes was content to ride with him in the matter.

'Well, sergeant, I'm Detective Superintendent Welling, this is Inspector Dykes, and Sergeant Prior over yonder. Sit down, both of you and let's be getting on. We're busy men in Whitsea and especially during the holiday season.'

He shuffled some papers in front of him and his frown deepened.

'It seems the presence of Regional Crime Squad members in the town hasn't had much influence yet,' he grunted. 'I've news for you Spratt. Another hotel robbery last night. The Burleigh, in Manor Road. Furs, jewellery, a couple of fat money wallets. Carried out, as before, when the guests were at dinner. Rooms entered, no locks forced, no prints, no evidence. Passkey or skeleton used, I s'pose.' He yawned, showing big, strong teeth. 'I was up most of the night. Well, you Deniston experts? Any suggestions?'

'Same M.O. as used in the other three hotel jobs we discussed last night,' Spratt commented. 'So you'll have checked the staff, of course, sir?'

Welling made a gesture of irritation. 'Of course we've checked the blasted staff. With no lead, as before. So we've got to look at the guests. Which my men are already doing. They won't get anywhere. As I said last night, it could have been done by a guest or guests who've stayed there previously and then checked out when they'd studied the layout and the general running of the place. And taken room key impressions, I shouldn't wonder. The staff can't keep tabs in these big places, on who's supposed to be still staying there and who isn't.'

Spratt nodded. 'We've already agreed these jobs are the work of a gang — they just couldn't have been done by a lone operator. We've no knowledge of any such gang in the North Central District, and the enquiry I put through to the Yard has proved negative. They rang me with that information this morning. We'll put it on to Interpol level, of course, but there may be some delay there.'

'Negative! Delay!' Welling grunted. 'It's action, something positive, we need. And don't forget those store robberies, either.'

'I have them in mind sir,' Spratt assured him. 'I've studied the files you gave me last night. Obviously, there was careful preparation for each one of these jobs. Again, the marks of gang work all over them.'

'And one gang doing both the hotels and the stores?' Dykes put in. Welling turned on him quickly.

'That doesn't follow, inspector. In my opinion, there are two gangs working here. You know as well as I do that the normal crook sticks to one line of country only. He doesn't touch store robberies if he's an expert on hotels.'

'One thing seems obvious,' Spratt said. 'One bunch or more, there's no peterman working here. None of the stores' safes were touched, the same goes for the hotels.'

'So where does that deduction get us, Spratt?'

'It could help, sir. We'll computerise all the evidence we can gather and it's quite likely we'll come up with something!'

'Computers!' Welling growled. 'Worst things ever loaded on to the police! When a C.I.D. man can't use his own brains, but has to rely on some blasted electronic machine, it's a poor do!'

'Excuse me, sir.' Detective Sergeant Prior poked his red head forward. 'I haven't had a chance to tell you yet, but I got a whisper this morning — '

A knock on the door interrupted him, and a young constable came in carrying a tray of coffee and a large plate of chocolate biscuits. Welling said, 'And about time, too, Liversidge! I thought you'd gone fishing off the pier again!'

This seemed to be some departmental joke, for even Dykes smiled, while Prior guffawed loudly and sycophantically. The constable who was awkwardly built, with large hands and feet, blushed furiously, clattered the tray on to the table and made a stumbling exit.

The coffee, or the biscuits, of which he ate an inordinate number, seemed to sweeten Welling's temper. He spoke quite pleasantly to Dykes.

'Any line on that Palladium hold-up, Charles?'

Dykes shook his head, and seeing Spratt's enquiring look, gave him the details of the box office robbery, without, however, mentioning Garrett's presence at the theatre.

'Well, keep trying,' Welling advised. 'That's one job you won't have to worry about,' he told Spratt. 'Me and my lads can handle that all right.'

'No connection, you think, with the big operators here?'

'Can't see any at the moment. If there is, we'll dig it out, you can be certain.'

'The woman in the paybox was threatened with a gun,' Spratt commented. 'And I read in your local evening paper last night of a shooting incident at a caravan site.'

'That point struck me right away,' Dykes said. 'But we have a very good description of the site gunman, and Mrs.

Graham, at the Palladium, was definite it didn't fit either of the men who cleaned her out.' He picked up a briefcase from the floor by his chair. 'By the way, sir,' he said to Welling, 'Fraser did me an excellent identikit picture of the site bloke. I've had it photo-copied and my men are showing it round the site, and the adjacent houses, this morning.'

He produced several copies and handed them round. 'Anybody you recognise, Mr. Spratt?' he asked.

'He's not known to me,' Spratt replied. 'Or to you?' he asked Garrett.

'No, sir.' Garrett studied the picture long and carefully. Could this possibly be the man he had heard blundering down through the cliffside bushes last night? Or could that marksman have been Read? He pushed his cup aside, deciding this was when he gave an account of his own adventure, though he wasn't sure how Welling would take the story.

'I was on that cliff path at the end of the promenade last night,' he said. 'About nine-thirty. I heard a shot, and the sound of a man running off down the slope, also a shout from another man . . . '

The superintendent's frown came back as Garrett continued his tale. At the end of it, Welling leaned across the table, bringing his hand down with a smack which made the empty cups rattle.

'And why the hell didn't you report this last night? What's the use of bleating it out to us now? You let this couple play a trick on you which a police cadet in his first week wouldn't have been taken in by, and yet you couldn't even bother to — Cor!'

He had a point, Garrett knew. He himself had been worrying over it. He'd meant to report the incident before returning home last night, and even his talk with young Colin Taylor, and the invitation from Dykes to come in on the Palladium job shouldn't have put it clean out of his mind. But, to face an undoubted fact, he'd forgotten, until he'd actually been going to bed. He'd thought of using the Whites' phone to the local station, had tried to force himself to make the call, but by then his leg was giving him so much gyp he just couldn't face dressing again, and staying up until a policeman came round and took down all the details. He'd salved his conscience by telling himself nothing could be done that night, anyhow.

But he couldn't explain all this to the angry Welling. He sat there, red-faced and uncomfortable, trying not to squirm in his chair, keeping silence because silence would serve him best.

It was Inspector Dykes who came to his aid.

'As it happened, if he'd made a report, it would just have had to go down on the pad, sir. The Palladium business had us at full stretch last night, as you know, and then the Burleigh Hotel robbery. No need to tell you that took up all the department's personnel — you were in the thick of it yourself, practically the whole of the night.'

The touch of flattery did its work. 'That's all very well,' Welling said in a more reasonable tone, 'but it was his duty to report, and I must say I'm much surprised — Hey, you, sergeant! If you were in Whitsea last night, and had time

69

to go up cliffs, how come you weren't at the conference with Mr. Hallam and the inspector here?'

'Let me explain,' Spratt put in. 'Sergeant Garrett is on sick leave here. He sustained a very serious injury when he tackled a killer who was armed with an axe — '

'I read about it!' Welling made the interruption with a flash of keen interest on his heavy features. And then, most surprisingly, he grinned, and stuck a large paw out across the table.

'Shake, lad! I'm right proud to meet you. I reckon that what you did took guts, and if you haven't already been recommended for the Police Medal, there's something wrong with the high-ups. Glad to be working with you! And I'm sorry what I said just now, about you letting that couple get away from you. With your handicap you could hardly have been expected — Say, what was this man like, the one who got shot at?'

Overwhelmed by Welling's praise and apology, Garrett had some difficulty in

70

recollecting details of the man on the cliff. But he did his best, and the result seemed to please Welling.

'Short and plump with a sort of nervous tic at one corner of his mouth when he talked, eh? Did he mention his war service at all? He did? Then I reckon I've got him.'

He turned to Spratt. 'Bloke named Theaker. One of these bar flies. He haunts the Prince's Hotel, the Three Crowns — places like that. Specialises in married women wanting an extra bit of fun — and there are plenty of those about amongst the visitors we get here. You know — husband's off fishing, or on the links, all day and spends his evenings drinking with his pals. Little woman's left on her own. Can you blame her for falling for such as Theaker?'

'No complaints from his conquests?'

'None. He has some of the foreshore concessions — bingo, amusement arcades and such — so he's not short of money. Just meets the women for fun. Anyway, I can lay my hands on him if it's necessary. So no harm done.'

And in a much more amiable atmosphere than formerly, they got down to a discussion of ways and means. Spratt promised to study the files of the hotel and store robberies exhaustively, he would go again over the ground already covered by the Whitsea men on the chance that a fresh eye might pick up a lead. Meanwhile, the resources of the Regional Crime Squad would be set to work, more men brought in to help the local C.I.D., detailed investigations of all guests who had stayed at the looted hotels, when or immediately before these had been 'done.' Welling, who had started with a definite bias against the Regional men, gradually accepted the fact that the large-scale operation deemed to be necessary was wholly outside the powers of his own pitifully-small staff. Under Spratt's tactful handling he changed from opposition to quite hearty acceptance.

'That's it, then,' he said at last. 'We'll co-operate, of course, inspector. I'll have a room made ready here for your use. And now you'll be wanting to get across to the Burleigh Hotel, no doubt, to see things for yourself. I don't think there's anything else, is there?'

Spratt grinned inwardly. Everything was sweetness and light here now. He hoped it would last.

'Only one point, sir. Just as the coffee was brought in, Sergeant Prior here was starting to tell you something. He never finished it. Some whisper you had, I think, sergeant?'

'Yes, sir.' He looked at Welling. 'From Puffer Tenby. He stopped me as I left here last night. Said he'd heard the word that one of the Whitsea banks was going to get done next. Nothing more — you know Puffer, sir. One sentence out of him, and you've had your lot.'

Welling made a note on his pad. 'Sure I know Puffer all right. Knew him before you started infant school, lad. Got him his first stretch, as a matter of fact. I'll warn the banks, but I'm willing to bet there's nothing in it. I hope you didn't part with much for — '

The intercom on his desk, behind the table, buzzed. Welling leaned back, stabbed a finger on a button. 'Yes?'

73

'Main desk, sir. There's a lad here who says he's just seen the fellow who did that shooting on the caravan site. He sounds quite genuine, too, sir. I thought Inspector Dykes should be told at once.'

5

'And what,' Mrs. Taylor had asked that morning, 'are you planning to do with yourself today, darling?'

She spoke in the bright, brittle manner of one making an attempt to smother the proddings of an uneasy conscience.

Her son Colin pushed his breakfast plate aside on the small caravan table, and met the question with one of his own.

'I suppose you and dad are playing golf again?'

'Well, we did think it might be rather a good idea. It's such a lovely day and we ought to take advantage of it, you know. I'll tell you what, dear. Why not come and walk round with us? Then we could all have lunch at the clubhouse — lovely, eh?'

'Not for me, mum, thanks. You know something? If there's one game I'll never want to play, or hear mentioned, in all my life, it's flippin' golf.'

Mrs. Taylor bent to peer into the small mirror set above one of the bunk beds.

'I expect you'll change your mind some day, darling,' she returned vaguely. 'Look, daddy says we ought to make an early start this morning — Sunday, you know. The course'll probably be crowded. And I see he has the car ready so if you'd be an angel and wash up and tidy round a bit before you go out . . . Oh, and you'll get lunch somewhere, won't you? I've put you some money out.'

Colin watched them drive off with a resignation which had become habit. They were all right, he supposed. As good as most fellows' parents, anyway. It was just that they weren't much in the way of companions on a holiday like this.

He did his chores, considering how to spend the day. A chap couldn't swim and sunbathe hour after hour. He was fed up with hanging around games of beach cricket and football, desperately hoping for an invitation to join in. In fact, the only bit of real fun he'd had since he came to Whitsea was trailing that chap Read from the caravan the previous evening. And even then he had to go and lose him! Anyway, he was glad the sergeant he'd met — Dick Garrett — had seemed to believe him when he'd said the gunman hadn't been dropped by the Kendalls outside the site. But why should they say that was what they'd done, when they hadn't?

It might be quite an idea to try to find out a little more about the Kendalls and the Reads this morning.

He locked the caravan with the spare key his father had put into his charge and walked casually across the site towards the entrance gates. When he drew level with the two caravans in which he was interested he saw the adult inhabitants of both were still at breakfast, but a small boy, some four years old, was kicking a large rubber ball about in front of the Reads' van.

The ball came shooting in Colin's direction. He trapped it with his foot, smiling at the youngster.

'That's my ball!' the boy said angrily. 'You send it back to me!'

'I'm just going to. Here, what's your

name? Mine's Colin.'

'Andrew Read sixteen Greenwood Avenue Deniston seven,' the boy said parrotwise. Colin remembered the days when he, too, was taught to repeat his name and address just like that. Very necessary, in case you got lost.

'Okay, Andrew, so let's play football.' He toed the ball gently back. 'Now you kick it hard at me — try to boot it right past me.'

Andrew took a mighty swing at the ball, missed it and sat down heavily. He shouted with laughter, scrambled up and succeeded in sending it a yard or two forward.

'That's fine!' Colin encouraged him. 'Back to me, now!'

Andrew's excited voice brought his father to the caravan door.

'What goes on? Oh, you're having a nice game, eh?' He looked Colin up and down. 'You a camper, too?'

'Yes, sir. We're down near the far end.'

'I see. Well, Andrew, don't tire yourself out, son. Mummy's taking you down to the beach soon.'

He withdrew into the van and shortly afterwards he and Mrs. Read came out and went into the caravan next door. Colin at once began to steer the game closer to the Sprite Musketeer. The two couples inside had begun an immediate discussion which sounded urgent, though he couldn't catch any words, only the tones of their voices. He slammed the rubber ball away past Andrew, far across the grass. The youngster trotted after it and Colin took the opportunity he had made to move closer to the van.

But it seemed the people inside were not to be taken by surprise. They must have been watching, for the talking stopped abruptly and Read opened the door and came out on to the portable steps.

'That's enough now, Andrew,' he called. 'Come on in here. Mrs. Kendall has something for you.' He turned to Colin. 'Thanks for amusing him, lad. Think he'll make a footballer one day?'

'He seems to have all the right ideas.'

'Good.' Read scooped the boy up, lifted him inside the van. Colin still stood there.

'Well, that's it, isn't it?' Clearly Read was wanting him to go. 'Be seeing you around, I expect, lad.'

'I was just wondering — how is Mr. Kendall this morning?'

'Oh, he's all right. It wasn't a bad wound, you know. I guess he was lucky.'

'Did you get the police round this morning with an identikit picture? We did.'

'So did we. They do a good job on these things.' Read moved impatiently. 'Well . . . '

This time Colin had to take the very broad hint. He wandered away, back in the direction of his own temporary home. Looking once over his shoulder, he saw Read going quickly out of the site gates. Opposite, across the road, was a public telephone box. Read went inside, began to dial.

'Hi, Colin! I was looking for you.'

It was Keith Jackson, the thirteen-year-old boy with whom he had made friends. Keith was fair-haired, plump yet always lively. 'You doing anything special this morning, Colin?'

'I'm never doing anything special — least, not while we're here. So what?'

'Well, my folks are going to church, but they've let me off that, seeing it's my holiday. And I wondered if you'd come for a walk with me.'

'Where to?' Colin asked cautiously. He knew Keith to be an anything-for-a-giggle type, who acted first and thought afterwards, often ruefully.

'Oh, just up the road for half an hour or so. There's a place I'd like to show you. I think you'll find it interesting.'

'What sort of place?'

Keith winked. 'You wait till we get there. I tell you, mate, it's something special. I was there with dad and mum yesterday evening, and I'm just dying to go again.'

Keith's mention of his parents cleared Colin's doubts. He knew them to be very staid, very proper people. Wherever or whatever this place was, it wasn't likely to lead, he thought, to any source of trouble.

'You've got yourself a deal,' he said.

They went out of the site, crossed the road and turned north. A mile farther on,

Keith led the way along a side road between the scattered houses of a new building development.

'It's just past this lot,' he said. 'You see, when we used to come to Whitsea, we always stayed at a guest house along here. That was before we got the caravan. It was a proper quiet place, this guest house, too quiet for me. I used to do a lot of exploring all round it.

'Well, last night the old folks felt like a walk, they decided to come along here and see if the guest house was still in operation. It is, but it's changed hands since we were there. Look!'

They had come to a wall on their right, with trees and tall bushes growing closely together behind it. Farther on, the wall was broken by a handsome pair of iron gates. These carried a board, newly painted. It announced, 'Healthways Guest House. Naturopathy. Massage. Remedial Gymnastics.' And in smaller letters, 'M. Pelford, Prop.'

'Is this what we've come to see?' Colin asked. The day had become very hot, the walk had made him tired and thirsty.

'That's it, mate. And d'you know why? Because this is one of these nudist places!'

Colin peered at the board again. 'It doesn't say so.'

'That's what naturopathy means, pin head! I heard dad tell mum last night when she asked him and he thought I wasn't listening.'

'So it's a nudist centre. Then what?'

'Well,' Keith said eagerly, 'I know this place like the back of my hand. A bit further along you can shin over the wall like smoke. You drop amongst a lot of bushes and you can get a super view of the house and gardens without being seen yourself.'

'Huh! So it isn't the house you've come all this way to see, with your tongue hanging out. You're hoping to get a look at the nudes — eh?'

Keith grinned. 'Only some of 'em. Can't say I'd be interested in the fellows. On a day like this, everybody'll be out in the grounds. It'll be a real lark!'

Colin frowned at him. 'It's not my idea of fun, spying on people like that. And we'd be in real trouble if we were caught.'

'Oh, come on, let's risk it. I know dozens of escape routes. Think of it — crowds of naked women!'

From the height of his superiority of one year in age Colin spoke loftily.

'Cuh! You dirty-minded little kids! Look, when you've seen one naked woman you've seen 'em all, believe me!'

'You mean you've — '

'Besides,' Colin cut in hurriedly, 'I'd have thought you'd have had plenty of that sort of thing on the beach. I mean, some of these girls, they don't leave much to the imagination, do they? You want to grow up a bit, son!'

But Keith was not to be discouraged.

'Listen, Colin. Apart from anything else, I've got my peashooter and a pocketful of ammo with me. Can you think of a better target than a nudist?'

'Can you think of a worse idea than getting caught and being hauled up before the beak on a charge of doing a Peeping Tom act? No, Keith, it just isn't on.'

Keith's face clouded. He scowled.

'Ah, get lost, misery!' He darted away, past the gates and, in the sure manner of one who knows from experience just where the finger and toe holds are, he began to swarm up the wall some thirty yards further on. Colin watched him reach the coping and swing lightly over. A glance through the gates showed the terraced frontage of a large house and nobody at all in sight. Shrugging, Colin followed Keith's route. He supposed he'd better keep an eye on the silly young twit.

He dropped by Keith's side into a clump of thick bushes. 'Changed your mind, eh?' the younger boy said. 'Come on, then, we'll move around till we get a view of the house.'

They threaded their way through the bushes and came to the edge of a big lawn. This swept up to one side of the terrace. Beyond the drive, on the other side, were flower borders, a large rockery, a pond with a statue in its centre.

The place seemed deserted except for a couple of middle-aged ladies, fully clad, who were parading briskly from end to end of the terrace and pausing at intervals with their hands on their hips to do deep-breathing exercises. Most of the house windows above the ground floor were closely curtained, as if the rooms they served were not in use. A tall, white-haired man came out of the open front door, took the steps at a single bound and strode lithely down the drive and out through the entrance gates.

Colin nudged his companion. 'No nudes. So let's get out of here before we're spotted.'

'There's a big, secluded sort of garden at the back of the house,' Keith replied. 'That's where they'll all be. And I know a way to it through these shrubberies so we needn't come out of cover at all.'

'I think we've come far enough,' Colin objected. 'This doesn't look like a nudist place to me — it's too open to the public view. In any case, as I said before, we'd be playing a dirty game, spying on 'em. There's another point, too.' He glanced at his watch. 'I'll have to be getting back to Whitsea. I've to have my lunch in the town and there's only one decent place — Haxley's — and you've to queue for ages if you don't get there in good time.'

'You please yourself what you do,' Keith answered. 'I'm going to have a look at that back garden.'

'Well, I'll stay here and give you ten minutes. After that I'm scarpering, mate.'

Keith made a face at him, grinned, and ducked away through the bushes. Colin retreated a little into deeper cover though he still had the house in view. Movement at one of the upper windows held his attention for some minutes but he couldn't see the person behind the glass. When he looked at the terrace again, the deep-breathing ladies had disappeared.

A man came round the side of the house from the direction in which Keith had headed. He was a tall, loose-limbed man who walked with his head thrust forward. Colin was conscious of a sudden surge of excitement. He couldn't see the man's features at all clearly, for his head was turned towards the house. The boy moved to the edge of the bushes, taking a chance on not being seen.

A dog came streaking from the terrace across the lawn, barking furiously, straight for Colin. He dodged back quickly. He wasn't afraid of dogs, and this specimen was by no means large — a brownish-black mongrel which, as it came nearer, he saw had no intention of attacking him. The dog was merely playful. It charged into the bushes, picked up a short piece of stick and, wagging its tail excitedly, dropped its burden at Colin's feet. Still barking, it waited for him to throw the stick.

Colin bent to pat the dog, but caresses were not what the mongrel wanted. His idea was a game, and he continued to say so, loud and long. Colin glanced up. The tall man he had seen, attracted by the noise, was now coming quickly across the lawn towards the bushes. For an instant, Colin saw him clearly.

Suddenly he stopped, turned away. He called out something which Colin couldn't distinguish, and was answered by a gruff voice somewhere on the boy's right. Colin decided this was where he made himself scarce. He picked up the stick, pitched it beyond a laurel bush, and as the dog darted away in search of it, he moved quickly back to the wall. Keith would have to look out for himself; it would do neither of them any good if he, Colin, were ignominiously captured as a trespasser.

The wall which had proved so easy to scale from the road presented quite a different problem on this side. There weren't any convenient holds as far as Colin could see. He ranged quickly along, and heard heavy footsteps coming nearer, boots crunching on gravel. A slightly-projecting stone offered a chance, Colin reached for it and heaved, his feet scrabbling desperately for a hold on the wall. He found one that would just bear him — and then came a tug on the welt of one of the sandals he was wearing. The dog, having retrieved the stick, had no intention of letting his new playmate get away from him. That tug unbalanced the boy, he dropped heavily to earth again.

And as he did so, a burly, wide-shouldered man came thrusting through the bushes. Colin was caught.

'And what d'you reckon you're doing here, then?' the man demanded angrily.

He had a dark, lowering face and he hadn't shaved that morning. He wore a stained boiler suit and a cap which had seen its best days. Colin pulled himself together. He was scared, but he'd have to try to talk himself out of this.

'Er — I wasn't doing any harm,' he said. 'Just a bit of exploring, that's all.'

The man growled an order to the still-barking dog, the animal fell silent and its master looked Colin over.

'You're no kid, just out for a bit of mischief,' he said. 'You're too old for that. Let's have the truth, now. What's the big idea?'

Colin swallowed hard and tried again.

'Well, the house there, you see, looked sort of interesting from the road and I thought I'd like a better view of it.' His voice trailed away before the man's sardonic grin. It was clear he wasn't going to be believed.

'This is private property, and I reckon you're up to something funny. So we'd better have a word with Mr. Pelford, who owns this place. But no, come to think of it, he's gone into Whitsea this morning.

So I'll take you to Mr. Canning instead.'

Colin was reckoning up his chances of rushing his way out of this situation. The trouble was, he was on strange territory and didn't know his way about. There were the entrance gates, of course, as a way of escape they offered a poor prospect, but as far as he could judge it was the only one available . . .

He balanced himself, ready for a quick dodging movement past the man. And then there came the sound of movement in the bushes and Keith appeared, grinning broadly.

'Well, what d'you know!' he exclaimed. 'My old friend Mr. Bailey! I was wondering if you were still here. How's everything with you?'

The man had swung round, and now his face broke into a beaming smile.

'Blow me down if it isn't young Keith! And up to your tricks again, I'll warrant! Say, is this chap a pal of yours, by any chance?'

'Sure he is. Colin Taylor. We're both on holiday at the caravan site at Whitsea. And this morning I thought I'd like to have a dekko at the old place again, but I could see it had changed hands so I said to Colin we'd nip over the wall, like I often used to — remember?'

Bailey chuckled. 'You bet! Proper young devil you always was. How's your mum and dad, then?'

'They're fine. And you're still working here, Mr. Bailey?'

'I am that. Sundays and all, too. But it's easy and they pay me well, y'know.'

Keith bent to make a fuss of the dog. 'I see you've still got old Buster.' He squinted up at the man. 'Say, Mr. Bailey, is it right this is a nudist place now?'

Bailey gave a snort of laughter. 'So that's what you two were up to? Well, you're right unlucky. Nothing of that sort here.'

'Then what is it exactly?' Colin asked.

'It's a sort of health centre. Folks come here and eat special diet, do exercises, have heat-ray treatment — all that. Me, I wouldn't want to spend a holiday that way — and be charged plenty for it, an' all.'

'What happened to Mr. and Mrs.

Sutton, who used to live here?' Keith queried.

'They retired, lad. Put the place up for sale. Mr. Pelford bought it last autumn and had it fixed up as a health centre. That's why there aren't many guests — or patients, if you like — yet. The place hasn't got known, you see.'

'Did you have any new people come in yesterday afternoon or evening, Mr. Bailey?' Colin asked.

'That I wouldn't know lad. I work outside, you see. People come and go but I don't keep track of them. The fellow who called out to me just now, that there seemed to be something in these bushes upsetting the dog — I've never seen him before. But he may have been here for a week or more for all I know. See, I think you two had better leave the way you came in — I'll give you a leg up over the wall. That way, we'll dodge any awkward explanations.'

When they were on the road again, nearing the town, Colin said, 'Did you get the cops round this morning, Keith, showing a picture of that chap who did the shooting yesterday?'

'Dad was saying something about it at breakfast. Actually, I wasn't up till later.'

'They came to us,' Colin said shortly, and then, 'Look, I'll see you later, eh? Sorry you didn't find any nudists, but it was a nice walk, and I did like your pal Bailey. Lucky it was he who caught me, as it turned out, eh?'

6

Little Mrs. Read turned away from the caravan window. 'He seems to have pushed off,' she said, 'but I don't trust that lad. I'm sure he was snooping around again this morning. He just made an excuse of playing with our Andrew so he could use those flapping ears of his. You're sure he wasn't actually following you last night, Denny?'

'Relax, Babs,' her husband advised. 'He was certainly behind me when I went down to the prom, but that was just chance, I'm sure. And even if it wasn't I shook him off, so why worry?'

He glanced at his watch. 'It's time I phoned Molly, like we arranged.' He looked across at the bandaged Kendall. 'I can tell her you're just about okay again Ivor?'

'You can tell her that even a flesh wound can be bloody painful.' Kendall moved uncomfortably, fingering his dressing. 'I'll be glad when it's time to go to the hospital again this morning. They put this lot on far too tight. Damn it, I can hardly breathe.'

'Molly's not going to be pleased,' Mrs. Read said gloomily. 'This business has mucked her plans up properly. That devil of a Ray Lever! I wonder where he's got to, anyway?'

'Back to Deniston, I shouldn't wonder,' her husband replied. He left the caravan and went to the telephone kiosk in the main road. He was back within three minutes.

'Molly's at the Burleigh Hotel, as you know,' he told the others. 'It was done last night, good and proper. Cops all over the place, usual questions, the lot. She didn't want to talk on the phone. I've to meet her in town, at the Carlton Cafe in Bridge Road. See you all later — I've got to hurry.'

He went out as he had come in — like a minor whirlwind. Dulcie Kendall stared after him.

'And I only hope he puts up a good tale to her about Ivor and Ray Lever,' she said. 'Molly can throw quite a bit of temperament when things don't go right.'

Dennis Read was thinking on identical lines as he drove his Triumph Herald into Whitsea. He had no apologies to make to Miss Molly Bilton on his own account, but he was betting she wouldn't be very pleased to hear the story of the caravan site shooting. He'd done what he could to make the best of a tricky business, he'd used his head and thought fast. Later reflections on his own actions had not altered his conviction that he'd done the right thing. But as he wove through the town-centre traffic he wondered how yesterday's incident would affect the plans laid so carefully over the past several months.

He was lucky enough to find a parking space near the Carlton Cafe. When he reached the cafe he saw it was doing a roaring mid-morning trade, but Molly, already there, had secured a table for two in a corner. He edged his way towards her, thinking that, wherever the place or whatever the circumstances, Molly Bilton stood out like a handsome plant in a bed of weeds.

She was tall, with a magnificent figure. Her hair was a rich chestnut, her eyes blue-grey, her mouth flawless. Her nose had a slight tendency to snubness; if this was an imperfection it merely emphasised the rest of her beauty. She looked good enough to eat, Read thought, and no doubt many a man in that cafe was envying him as he sat down with her. Little did they know — he wouldn't have accepted Molly on a golden platter as more than a companion. He knew her too well.

She had a cup of coffee in front of her and at once signalled for one to be brought to him. It arrived on the table almost before they had exchanged greetings. Molly never had to wait for service. 'How's that for a stroke of bad luck, Denny?' she began. 'I book in at an hotel and it gets knocked off before I've hardly unpacked! I'm telling you, that really rocked me!'

Read grinned. 'One you'd planned to do yourself, too. That's adding insult to injury, I reckon.'

'Well, fortunately they were only local

dicks who did the questioning, so no suspicions of yours truly. But it does look as if some other low-down crooks have had the same idea as we have. And that could complicate things.'

'You think it was a gang steal, then?'

'It had all the signs. Of course, I could be wrong and this was just a single effort. But there was a hold-up at the theatre ticket-office here last night, I'm told, and that Burleigh Hotel isn't the only one which has had trouble here lately. And there were those two store clean-out jobs. I'm beginning to think, Denny, that we've come here to find ourselves second in the field — not first.'

'And where does that leave us?'

Molly's lovely face was suddenly grim.

'In there and fighting, boy.' She leaned forward. 'Look, if we play our hand right, it may mean extra tricks if there's some other operator around. What we pull gets blamed on him, see? And I'll tell you something else. Not one of the jobs which have been done here have included safes. Which means Mr. Whoever hasn't got a peterman. But we have. One up to us.'

Read took a long swallow of coffee.

'Correction, Molly. Not 'we have.' 'We had.''

She stared across the table at him, her eyes hard.

'What the hell do you mean by that?'

'Now, look.' Read spoke placatingly. 'It was just one of those things. If it had been anybody else but Lever — ' He caught the impatience in her face and continued hurriedly.

'Ivor and Dulcie picked up Ray Lever at Pickering, as arranged. The idea, as you know, was to bring him here, check the plans with Barbara and me, and then Ivor was to run him on to that boarding house where he had booked in. Okay, they arrive at the site and park next to us. Ivor starts getting stuff out of the car, Dulcie says she'll make a cup of tea if Ray'll connect up the calor. After a bit, Ivor hears Dulcie yelling for him so he nips into the van. And there's Ray trying on a bit of hot smooching with Dulcie. You know how he is when he gets within armslength of an attractive bird.'

'Go on, for Pete's sake, man!'

'Ivor was mad, of course — who wouldn't be? He hit Lever and what did that dope do but pull a gun on him!'

'A gun? I didn't know Ray Lever carried one!'

'Nor did we, but facts are facts, Molly. Ivor, still blowing his top, went to get the gun off him, and Lever pulled the damn trigger. Ivor had the narrowest escape of his life. The bullet grazed his neck, not deeply, but a nasty job all the same.'

'My God! The duff stuff I have to work with!'

'Babs and I heard the shot,' Read continued. 'I rushed into the other van. Dulcie was nearly in hysterics, Ivor was collapsed and bleeding and I just caught a glimpse of Lever dodging away across the site. Ivor had managed to grab the gun, I picked it up and shoved it in my pocket. And then, of course, Dulcie had to rush across to the warden's office screaming for an ambulance. Not that I blame her,' he added. 'Ivor really needed attention.'

His companion shrugged in disgust.

'And the next thing you knew, the dicks were swarming all over the place.

Go on, let's have it all!'

'I did the best I could. I gave Ivor and Dulcie a tale to tell the cops and this seems to have gone over okay.' He repeated the statement the Kendalls had made to the police about the man to whom they had given a lift, who had, they said, followed their caravan on to the site and had demanded money at gun point. Molly nodded in grudging approval.

'The question is,' she said, 'what happened to Lever? You've not seen him since?'

'No, but I've been trying to look at things from his point of view. He may be a wizard on safes but you can't credit him with much intelligence, you know. If he hadn't panicked, probably thinking he'd done Ivor properly, we could have patched something up. But it would be expecting too much to imagine he'd stop for a moment and think that out. No — cut and run, that's just about his thought-limit. Now he knows the cops are after him. So, in my book, he ducks back to Deniston. That's where you'll have to look for him, Molly, if you still want to use him.'

'If the cops don't find him first. He could still be on the dodge somewhere in Whitsea.'

'Which is what we want the said cops to think, isn't it? While they're busy looking for him — and they've got a really good identikit of him they're showing around — they won't have time to wonder about us.'

Molly drew a sharp breath. 'Identikit picture? Who gave them the details for that?'

'Dulcie. Oh, I know what you're thinking — that she should have weighed in with a phoney description. But there was Ivor, apparently bleeding to death, and Dulcie in a panic about him, and wanting the man who had shot him to be collared. That's only natural, isn't it?' But as he said it, he doubted whether a woman like Molly Bilton knew what 'natural' meant in such circumstances. He had the feeling he was talking a foreign language to her. 'One thing,' he went on, 'Dulcie did say the chap they were supposed to have given a lift to came from Leeds. Which means he'll be looked for there, and not in Deniston.'

Molly put her elbows on the table, cupping her chin in her hands.

'It's all one blasted mess, whichever way you look at it,' she muttered. 'And it'll need some thinking out.' She was silent for some moments and then seemed to come to a decision.

'Denny, you check on that boarding house Ray Lever was booked in at. It's just possible he's lying low there — it's the sort of thing that dumb cluck would do. If you find him, tell him from me to get back to Deniston quick. I'll contact him there. If he hasn't ducked in at the boarding house, I'll get our Deniston crowd to see if they can dig him up.' She swung to her feet. 'Come on, we'd better go.'

'I'll ring your hotel when I've been to the boarding house?'

'Better not. I'll come along to that caravan site this afternoon and we'll all have a proper conference. My car has had to go into dock here, but you're not far out of town. After all, we've no definite plans worked out yet here, so a day or two's delay won't harm us.'

'There's just one other thing you ought to know — ' Read was beginning, but he was talking to Molly's back. In her imperious manner she was already half-way to the door. Read shrugged and picked up the bill the waitress had laid beside his coffee cup. Molly never wasted time on formal goodbyes.

But as he turned away from the cash desk he saw her move quickly back from the door. She opened her bag and took a purse from it, turning towards a fruit machine just inside the entrance, as if she had suddenly made up her mind to take a chance on sixpence.

'I shouldn't have thought these things would have interested you,' Read said, coming up to her as she dropped a coin into the slot. Molly, as he knew her, was certainly one of life's gamblers, but on the big issues only. Small jobs, small winnings, simply had no place at all in her philosophy.

She pulled down the handle, the small painted discs whirled in a tripartite blur.

Then Read saw she was not even looking at the machine, her eyes, alert and hard, were on the street beyond the door. She turned to him as the whirring stopped.

'Queue of cars held up at those traffic lights,' she murmured. 'Take a look. There's the local C.I.D. inspector driving one of them. He has a young lad in front with him, and in the back, who but that sergeant from the Deniston regional crime squad. Garrett — that's his name. So what's he doing here, and what does it mean to us?'

Read darted to the door and saw for himself. He had never made Garrett's acquaintance, but he knew the young lad in the car all right.

7

Colin Taylor got rid of his friend Keith Jackson with a distinct feeling of relief. The exciting discovery he had made while waiting for Keith in the bushes had been bubbling in the forefront of his mind all the way back to Whitsea. He had had to stop himself firmly, several times, on the point of telling Keith. Which wouldn't have been at all wise, for there was always the chance that he, Colin, had been mistaken, in which case he'd look an awful ass in front of his holiday pal.

Now it was a matter of handing on what he believed, and hoped, to be vital information. The best thing would be to go straight to the central police station. He lengthened his stride, heading in that direction.

But he found it somewhat intimidating to climb the broad flight of steps, to push through the main doors and to find himself facing a short counter behind which an officer was busy with a telephone. But as Colin came up to the counter, the man put the phone down, made a note on a pad and said, 'Well, what is it?'

Nervousness brought Colin's words out jerkily.

'Er — I'm from the caravan site, I mean, we're camping there. That shooting yesterday — the police came round this morning with an identikit picture. I saw it — I mean, they showed it to us — my parents and me.'

The officer sighed wearily. 'Come to the point, lad.'

'Sorry. But I saw the man this morning — I mean, I'm almost sure I did. At a sort of guest house. It's off the Northway Road and it's called Healthways.'

'And you thought you'd better report this to us, eh? That was the proper thing to do. Only, are you absolutely sure about this? You got a really good look at him — you couldn't be mistaken?' He picked up his pencil again. 'Anyway, let's have the details.'

As briefly as he could, Colin told the

story of his adventure with Keith Jackson that morning. The man behind the desk listened more attentively as the tale proceeded.

'Well,' he said when Colin came to an end, 'it's quite possible we've got something here. You and your pal were trespassing' — he grinned — 'with evil intent. So if you hadn't been pretty sure about this chap, I reckon you wouldn't have come here to report, would you? You'd have wanted to keep quiet about your trip this morning.

'Now, look. Inspector Dykes, who's in charge of that shooting job, is on the premises. How about telling this yarn all over again to him?'

'I'd be glad to,' Colin agreed, and was shown into a room with the inspector's name on the door. Inside two minutes Dykes appeared, and Colin's face lit up when, behind Dykes, he saw Sergeant Garrett.

'Ah!' Garrett greeted him pleasantly. 'We've met before. Inspector, Colin Taylor's by way of being a pal of mine.'

'Which makes things nicer all round,

doesn't it?' Dykes responded. He settled them in chairs and went to sit behind his own desk. 'Now, Colin, let's have it.'

Colin had lost his nervousness now. He hadn't liked the task of admitting to the reception officer why he and Keith had been to Healthways, but the man had taken it all right, and a second telling didn't seem to make it any worse, though Dykes and Garrett exchanged brief smiles when they heard of Keith Jackson's hopes. Colin hated the idea of splitting on Keith, but it had to be done and he was sure nothing more would be said about it.

'We haven't had any luck yet in our enquiries about this man,' Dykes said when Colin fell silent. 'In fact, yours is the only lead which has turned up.' He glanced at his watch. 'I've time to make a call on this Healthways place, I think. Maybe you'd care to come along, Colin? Identification, you know, in case we see the man again. And you, sergeant?'

Garrett nodded enthusiastically and Colin sprang up at once. He wasn't going to miss a chance like this; as for the

110

business of his lunch, that could be shelved for the moment.

They went with Dykes to the official car park behind the building. Garrett eased himself into the rear seat of a well-kept Consul and Dykes, at the wheel, had Colin beside him. Despite a hold-up at a set of traffic lights, they made good time out of the town. Dykes needed no directions to find Healthways, he knew his district thoroughly. The entrance gates were standing open, Dykes drove to the front door and parked his car on a gravelled area which was occupied by a shining, bright-red Saab.

'You stay in the car, Colin,' Dykes said. 'We're going to make some preliminary enquiries and we'll call you in if necessary.'

Followed by Garrett, he walked up the entrance steps and rang the bell. It was answered, very promptly, by a young woman in a freshly-laundered, dazzlingly white overall. She was above average height, she had smooth, shining dark hair, an oval face attractively fragile-looking and a deep tan which suggested sunshine rather than the contents of a bottle. She raised well-marked eyebrows interrogatively.

'Good morning. I'm Detective Inspector Dykes.' He flicked out a card. 'This is Detective Sergeant Garrett. We'd like to speak to the proprietor, if we may.'

The girl's eyes went from one to the other of them. She hesitated for a long moment.

'Mr. Pelford had to go into Whitsea this morning. I'm not sure if he has returned. If you'd care to wait inside . . . '

She stepped back to let them enter a large, sunny hall, parquet-floored, its white-painted walls gleaming. She went away through a door at the far end of the hall, which, a few seconds later, was opened again by a short, stoutish man in his mid-fifties, with a rosy face below a thatch of crisp, silvering hair. He wore heavy rectangular-framed spectacles, and his dark suit and tie, his white shirt and highly-polished shoes gave him an immaculately-professional appearance.

'Good morning, gentlemen.' The voice was deeply pitched, pleasantly vibrant.

'My name is Pelford. What can I do for you?'

Dykes went through the process of self-identification again.

'You may be aware, sir, of a shooting incident which took place at the caravan site on Northway Road yesterday?'

'Ah, yes, there was a report in the evening paper.'

'We have information that the gunman was seen on your premises here this morning.'

Pelford's head jerked up. 'Here? But you surely can't mean that? And yet . . . ' He glanced out of the window at the extensive grounds which surrounded the house. 'I suppose there is a certain amount of cover available out there for a man — er — on the run. This is quite alarming, gentlemen. I think we'd better continue our discussion in my office.'

He led the way through the door by which he had entered the hall into a small room, oak-panelled and somewhat severely furnished with a flat-topped desk, several tubular-steel chairs and a metal filing cabinet. There was a telephone on the desk, with a couple of wire trays, both empty, a stationery rack and a blotter with covers of tooled leather. Pelford waved his visitors to seats and sank into a swivel chair behind the desk.

'You think he may be still hiding on the premises?' he asked. 'You would like to organise a search? I assure you, we will do everything we can to assist.'

'Our information, sir, was that the man was walking in the grounds quite openly, as if he were a guest here.'

'But that's quite impossible, inspector! I have been away from the house this morning, but my staff would surely have seen an intruder about the place and would have taken whatever action was necessary.'

'What have you in the way of staff here, sir?'

'There is Miss Henson, our receptionist and housekeeper. You have already met her. There is Mr. Canning, my assistant. He is our physiotherapist. A local man named Bailey does our maintenance work and looks after the garden. His wife assists in the kitchen. We have a cook, and two women who come in daily as cleaners.'

'Guests?'

'At the moment, only a Mrs. Green and her sister Miss Lodge, and a Mr. Hillyard.'

'Not very many for a place this size,' Dykes remarked drily.

Pelford made a small grimace. 'It is a fact that at the moment our numbers are small. But you see, inspector, this is no ordinary guest house. We specialise in health treatments — dieting, sun-rays, remedial gymnastics, massage, sauna baths. I bought this house last year, so this is our first season and we haven't got fully started yet. Such an establishment as this depends on personal recommendations, you know. I shall build it up over the coming years, I trust.'

He brought his hands down upon his desk. 'But, look here, you haven't come to indulge in chat, have you? Hadn't we better do something about this intruder who may be still around?'

Dykes nodded. 'Of course. I'd like to ascertain if any of your guests or staff saw him. Would this be possible, sir?'

'Nothing easier. I'll have them sent in here to you.'

Pelford sprang up. 'You would like to question them separately, I suppose?'

'It's usually best in these cases, sir.'

'Very good. I'll be as quick as I can.'

He hurried out, closing the door behind him. Dykes turned to Garrett.

'Well, sergeant, what do you make of it all?'

Garrett frowned thoughtfully. 'I don't quite know. Pelford seems genuine enough, and yet . . . There's something a bit odd somewhere, but I can't put my finger on it.' He shrugged. 'A sort of phoney atmosphere. Maybe it's — '

He broke off, and both men got to their feet as the dark-haired receptionist came in. Garrett began to move a chair forward but the girl waved the offer away and perched herself, swinging her handsome legs, on the edge of the desk.

'I'm Gaye Henson,' she said. 'Martin — Mr. Pelford — says you want to ask some questions. I'll do what I can to help, of course.'

'Thanks, Miss Henson.' Dykes took out a copy of the identikit picture and handed it to her. 'Do you recognise this man?'

She gave the picture a superficial glance, shook her head and then, in the act of handing the sketch back, she stopped herself and examined it closely. Then she laid it down on the desk at her side.

'Do you know,' she said slowly, 'I think I have seen him. This morning, somewhere around ten o'clock.' She turned her head to look at the picture again. 'Yes, I'm certain it was the same man.'

'Please tell us all about it, Miss Henson.'

'I was in what we call the sun room — it's a lounge used by the guests — I was giving it a general tidying up. Just outside it there's a short passage which leads to a side door into the grounds. I heard somebody knocking at this door. I went to see who it was, and found a man standing there.

'I asked him what he wanted, of course,

and he said he'd like to enquire about our terms for resident guests. I invited him in to the sun room, which was empty, and gave him one of our brochures. He said he was staying in Whitsea, but liked the look of the guest house and thought he might try a holiday here sometime in the future.'

'Did he seem quite normal? Not unduly worried nor uneasy?'

'If you mean, did he look like a man on the run, I'd say definitely no. For instance, he'd shaved this morning because I noticed he'd a slight cut on his chin which was newly done.'

'Good observation,' Dykes commented. He took out his notebook. 'Now, would you describe him for me, please? What he was wearing, details about his personal appearance.'

Miss Henson's well-marked brows drew together as she concentrated.

'I'd put him in his early forties. He had brown hair — he wasn't wearing a hat. He was fairly tall, just over six feet, I'd say. He had an open-necked white shirt, a russet-coloured sports coat and brown slacks.'

'Shoes?'

'I didn't notice them, I'm afraid.'

'Anything else about him? Accent? Eyes? Teeth?'

'He spoke good English without any particular accent. I can't tell you the colour of his eyes, and his teeth were — well, now I come to think of it, he could have been wearing dentures but very often you can't tell these days, can you?'

'You say he came to the side door. That was unusual for a caller, surely?'

'It was. I asked him why he hadn't rung the front door bell and he said he'd had a fancy to stroll round the grounds first before he made enquiries. And that's about all. I let him out at the side door again and watched him go off round the house in the direction of the front drive. Oh, I did notice he walked in a shambling sort of way, with his head forward. I remember thinking that Bert Canning, our P.T. instructor here, would want to put him through some remedial exercises, if he'd seen him, to teach him to walk better.'

Dykes looked up from the notes he had been making.

'Thank you very much, Miss Henson. You've been most helpful. We needn't detain you any longer.'

She was in the act of sliding down from her perch on the desk when her employer, after a tap on the door, came in again.

'My grilling's completed,' she told him. 'Who's next?'

Pelford waved her out of the room before he turned to his visitors.

'I've been trying to save you some time, gentlemen. None of the staff saw this man, neither did our two lady guests. Mr. Hillyard, our other guest, has gone into town this morning, so he's out of it. Of course, if you would still prefer to see everybody personally, I will ask them to come in here.'

'In the circumstances, sir, I think we can dispense with further interviews since you've questioned these people yourself.' Dykes added casually, 'As it's Sunday, your gardener would not be working?'

Pelford slapped a hand to his forehead.

'Bailey! I completely forgot him! And he is working here this morning. He took a day off last Tuesday to go to a local show, so he's making up for that by working today. I'll send for him.'

'No need for that, sir. We'll have a talk to him on our way out.' Both policemen were on their feet and Dykes turned to the door. 'You've been most co-operative and helpful, sir.'

Pelford smiled. 'But naturally, inspector. And one can only hope this man you are looking for is safely in your hands before he does any more damage. I will see you out.'

He opened the front door for them, walked out behind them on to the steps. 'Ah,' he said, 'there's the man you want.' He raised his voice. 'Bailey! Can you come a moment, please?'

The gardener turned slowly as he straightened up from the flower bed he was weeding. The brownish-black dog which lay near him sprang to its feet at the call, but the man spoke to it and it lay down again. Bailey walked leisurely across the lawn towards the house, rubbing his hands on the seat of his boiler suit.

'Nice-looking job, that.' Garrett gestured at the red Saab on the gravel in front of the steps.

'I'm rather pleased with it,' Pelford responded. 'It's the first time I've had a foreign car and I haven't really tested this one out yet — it's still at the running-in stage. But up to the present I haven't been able to fault it.' His glance went to Colin, still seated in the Consul. 'I didn't realise you had somebody else with you, inspector. You should have brought him in.'

'Oh, he's just a young friend, come for the ride, sir.' Bailey had joined them now, and both police officers noted his slight hesitation and his look of surprise as he walked past the Consul and saw Colin.

'These gentlemen are police from Whitsea, Bailey,' Pelford said. 'They have been informed that a wanted man has been hanging about the grounds here this morning. Have you seen any strangers around?'

'The only people I've seen,' Bailey answered stolidly, 'was Mr. Hillyard going out for his usual long walk, and then two ladies as are staying here. And another fellow who came out of the house and then went back again. Stranger to me, he was, but I took it he was another guest — a new one.'

'What was he like, Mr. Bailey? Would you describe him in detail, please?' Dykes asked.

Bailey pushed his cap to the back of his head and scratched an ear reflectively.

'Tallish, no hat, brown hair — I think. At any rate, it was neither very dark nor yet very fair. Middle-aged man. Brown coat and trousers.' He glanced at Pelford. 'That right, sir?'

Pelford laughed shortly. 'I wouldn't know, Bailey. He wasn't a guest here, you see. Did you speak to him?'

'What happened was this. I'm working on that flower bed — been at it all morning — and old Buster, my dog, is with me. Suddenly he jumps off and runs into the shrubbery yonder, barking like hummer. I look up and I see this fellow coming round the side of the house. He calls out to me something like, 'What's that in the bushes making the dog bark?' Well, I know Buster. Silly old devil has a habit of going for hedgehogs, and can't learn he's bound to get the worst of it with them. So I leaves me work and goes to the dog. I couldn't see no hedgehog in yon shrubbery, so I fetched Buster out and when I'd done so this fellow had gone — back into the house, I thought.'

He shrugged, clearly having to come to the end of his story.

'While you were in the shrubbery,' Dykes said, 'could this man have concealed himself somewhere else in the grounds?'

Bailey scratched his ear again. 'I suppose so. Or he could have walked out of the front gates, come to that.'

Garrett — and Dykes — noticed he answered the question in a different tone of voice from the one he had used to relate his story. Then, he had spoken loudly, almost stridently, now his voice was pitched at a normal conversational level.

Pelford turned to the policemen. 'A search, inspector? There are four of us here — five if your young friend would help — and Mr. Canning would also join us. To say nothing of the intrepid Buster,' he added with a chuckle.

Dykes shook his head. 'I think not, sir. If it was the man we're looking for, I doubt if he'd still be hanging around. Actually, it was probably a case of mistaken identity. We get them all the time, you know.'

They wished Pelford and Bailey good-day and went to Dykes' car. As soon as they were clear of Healthways, the inspector gave Colin an outline of what they had been told. The boy's face became glum.

'I'm sorry, Mr. Dykes. Only, you see, I was sure . . . I mean, I'd studied that identikit picture and I know I've a good visual memory. Now you'll be mad at me for bringing you out here on a wild goose chase.'

'Forget it,' Dykes said kindly. 'We had to make sure, you know.' He negotiated the right-hand turn into Northway Road and smiled. 'Your friend Bailey was very loyal, wasn't he? He was obviously surprised to see you in this car, but he made sure he said nothing to get you into trouble, and he took care you could hear what he was saying to Mr. Pelford, eh?'

'Yes,' Colin agreed. 'Of course, he was doing it for Keith Jackson's sake, not mine. He doesn't really know me.'

At the boy's request they dropped him at the gates of the caravan site. Dykes drove on for a short distance, turned the car into a side road and stopped.

'You'll be wanting to get back to your boarding house for lunch,' he said to Garrett. 'I know we've passed it, but I can run you back. I wanted a word with you when we'd got rid of the boy. You think he was mistaken about seeing our gun-toter?'

'It begins to look like it, sir. Though there were one or two odd points which struck me at that Healthways place.'

Dykes nodded. 'The red Saab, standing on the drive where that Henson girl couldn't have failed to see it when she opened the door to us. Yet she made out she wasn't sure if Pelford had got back. Nice fishing of yours, by the way, making certain it was Pelford's car . . . Point is, did she put up the yarn to give her time to consult Pelford, so that some plan — some explanation to us — could be made about this so-called mysterious visitor?'

'And Bailey would have seen him if he had come in from the road, sir, for he was working quite close to the gates.'

Dykes nodded, and pressed the starter switch. 'Yes, Healthways could do with a bit of watching — if I can find the time, and the men, for the job!'

8

Before leaving Dennis Read, earlier that Sunday morning, Molly Bilton had decreed that a conference at the caravan site would, after all, be unwise. If this nosy youth who seemed to be interested in her colleagues, and who was in touch with the police, saw her there with the Reads and the Kendalls, he might get an unfortunate impression of her — unfortunate from her point of view, of course. So she changed the venue of the meeting to a place where they could all talk in perfect isolation and secrecy. They would have their get-together on one of the most crowded parts of the sands.

So there they were, an apparently innocent group amidst dozens of other groups, with a hired canvas windbreak and five deck chairs, Dulcie and Barbara in bikinis, soaking up the sun, and Dennis Read in trunks doing likewise. Ivor Kendall, discharged from hospital outpatient care that morning, with a lightweight highnecked sweater concealing the plaster strip over his flesh wound, lounged in one of the chairs with a crumpled Sunday newspaper on his knees. Young Andrew Read was busily constructing a sand castle, totally absorbed in the job. And Molly, looking cool and model-like in a trim apple-green dress and a deep-brimmed cream canvas hat, sat in the centre to complete the picture of a family party.

Read, face downwards on a spread towel, spoke without looking up.

'So, as I've told the rest, Molly, he didn't turn up at the digs you booked for him.'

'I'll ring Sam, in Deniston, this evening,' Molly said. 'If Ray Lever's bolted back there, Sam and his boys'll find him.'

'And bring him back here, I hope,' Kendall grunted. His hand went up to his neck. 'I want to have a word with Lever — after I've kicked most of his teeth down his throat, of course.'

'You can skip that line of talk,' Molly

told him crisply. 'I'll deal with Lever, and he won't be jumping for joy when I've done so, either.'

'Even if you find him, you can't bring him back here, you know, Molly,' Barbara Read said. 'The cops would finger him at once.'

'I agree,' Molly said grimly. 'Thanks to Dulcie's most accurate description of him.'

Mrs. Kendall's head came up sharply.

'Now, look, I thought Ivor had had it proper, and — '

'Yes, yes, I know, dear. You acted quite like a natural and loving wife. You were shocked and frightened and you just hadn't the presence of mind to hand out a false description. If you had, we'd have no problems, once we find Lever. I suppose, though, it's hardly fair to blame you.'

'And you'd better not, either, Molly,' Ivor Kendall said, quietly now. 'Supposing Dulcie had given a completely phoney description, and Lever had been picked up because somebody else had seen him charging out of our van, and had kept an eye on him? Dulcie would have had a nasty bit of explaining to do then.'

'All right, all right! Forget it.' Molly waved her hands. 'What's done is done. It's the future we've got to think about.'

'Me,' Dennis Read said, 'I don't see we've got any future here. We made certain plans for Whitsea. For them, we needed a first-class peterman. So you, Molly, bring Lever in. Now we've lost Lever, and his services. Let's call the whole idea off, I say.'

'You can forget that, too,' Molly snapped. 'I told you this morning, it's my belief there's another lot operating here already, which makes it all the better for us, once you see it my way. I admit, with Lever out of it, we may meet a few extra difficulties, but what of it? My old dad always used to say difficulties were made to be got over and I go along with that all the way.' She rose gracefully to her feet. 'I've got a little job to do, you know, up at your camp site. With luck, I'll meet up with your young friend there.'

'Well, he seemed all settled for the afternoon when we left.' Read grinned.

'And I don't give much for his chances when you start the old pump-handle act, either. We'll see you later, then?'

'I'll be in touch.' Molly waved and turned away to the steps which led to the promenade. Dulcie Kendall watched her.

'Baby-snatching, just her line,' she said sourly. 'Oh, to hell with it all. I wish — '

'Come on, you girls,' Read broke in. 'Down to the briny. It's time those costumes, what there is of them, got wet.'

*   *   *

Colin Taylor had decided, when Inspector Dykes had put him down at the site gates, that he wouldn't bother fagging back into the town for lunch. By then, the queues at all the eating places would be miles long, it just wouldn't be worth the trouble to try for a decent meal. He crossed the road to the snack bar where he had spent time the previous afternoon. This was busy, too, but the service was brisk, and he hadn't to wait long before he was able to buy a packet of crisps, a meat pie, and a bottle of Coca-Cola. He carried these back to the caravan, found a packet of chocolate biscuits and a plate, and set a canvas chair outside in the sunshine.

As he was settling down to his meal, the Kendalls and the Reads came across the grass between the parked vans, heading for the small gate which led down to the sands. Their route took them past at some little distance from him, but they all glanced in his direction and Read raised a hand in greeting. Colin waved back.

He had finished eating, and was glancing through a magazine when a pleasant voice addressed him.

'Excuse me butting in, but I wonder if you could possibly help me?'

Colin looked up with a start, at a woman in a green dress who carried a wide-brimmed sun hat in one hand. She had chestnut-coloured hair, and though to Colin she was rather old — which to his way of thinking meant anybody over twenty — she was undoubtedly a smasher. He scrambled to his feet.

'Of course — if I can. What's the trouble, exactly?'

'I've lost a rather valuable brooch, somewhere around here, I think.' She had come close to him and a slim finger indicated two tiny holes in the material of her dress, where a brooch pin had been fastened. 'You see? And I feel sure it fell off when I came across here this morning.'

'I haven't come across a lost brooch,' Colin said. 'But I'll help you to search, if I may.'

'Oh, but I couldn't put you to that trouble. I'll just hunt around, if you don't mind me bursting in on your privacy.'

'But I'll be glad for something to do,' Colin assured her. 'And I'm a jolly good finder of things. Somewhere about here, you think?'

'Yes. You see, I was down on the beach this morning and somebody told me I could reach Northway Road by taking the little path yonder and crossing this site. Actually, I suppose, I shouldn't have come on here at all, because it is private to you caravan people, isn't it? But I was in a dreadful hurry to get back to my hotel in time for lunch, and I knew I could catch a convenient bus on the main road yonder. So I came the nearest way.

'Well, I know I had the brooch when I came through the gate there and I noticed it was gone when I was on the bus. I didn't lose it there, so . . . It was too late to turn back and look for it here then, so I thought I'd retrace my steps this afternoon and hope for the best. I expect it'll have been picked up before now, though.'

'In which case it may have been handed in at the site warden's office. We'll try there if we don't find it around here. Just where did you walk across?'

'I came straight in this direction from the little gate for some distance, and then I detoured round several of these vans.'

'We'll just nose around here for a bit first, then. Everybody seems to have gone out for the afternoon, so nobody'll mind. You go that way, I'll go this.'

As Colin had claimed, he was a good finder. Within a couple of minutes he saw a sparkle in the grass between his parents' caravan and the one directly behind it. He dived down and gave a yell of triumph.

'Here you are! Hit the jackpot first time!'

The woman came hurrying to him. 'That's my brooch, certainly. My initials in brilliants on it — see, M.B. — Molly Brown.' She gave a long sigh of relief. 'I just don't know how to thank you. Please tell me your name.'

'Colin Taylor. I say, I am glad I found it, Miss Brown.'

'Just call me Molly, Colin.' She passed the back of her hand across her forehead. 'I thought my brooch had gone for good. D'you know — it's reaction, I suppose, but I've gone all shaky.'

'Reaction and the hot day,' Colin said promptly. 'You come and sit down for a minute or two, and you'll be okay again.'

'You really are a perfect angel, Colin.' She followed him round the caravan and sank thankfully into the canvas chair. 'If I'm not being too much of a nuisance . . .'

'Of course not! Look, I'll just tidy this plate and things away and then I'll put the kettle on in the van. A cup of tea will just set you up.'

'But I couldn't possibly put you to such trouble — really!'

Colin waved her protests aside. He darted into the caravan, set the kettle going on the calor gas stove and busied himself preparing a tea-tray. Within a few minutes he had a table set up outside and Molly was pouring tea for them both — just, Colin thought, as if she had been his mother.

'You seem to be on your own,' she said as she lifted her cup.

'Dad and mum are golfing fans.' She was so easy to talk to; in no time he was pouring out all his boredom to her, and revelling in the sympathetic way she reacted to him.

'Do you know,' she said as she passed his refilled cup, 'I'm sure I've seen you before somewhere — quite recently, too.'

'In the town, or on the sands, perhaps,' Colin suggested. 'I've been around all last week, you know.'

'I've got it!' Molly clapped her hands. 'This morning, as I was coming out of the Carlton Cafe in Bridge Road. You were in a car — it was halted at the traffic lights

— with two men. I thought you said you hadn't made any friends here besides this boy Keith Something?'

'Those two were policemen,' Colin responded, with more than a touch of pride. 'C.I.D., to be exact. I was helping them on a job.'

'You were? But this is most exciting. Do tell me!'

And Colin told her. Every detail. About the man he'd seen at Healthways, and how he'd reported to the police. 'So they took me with them,' he ended, 'but it was all a washout. I mean, we had the journey for nothing. Yet I'm sure it was the man — I'm certain of it.'

'The detectives wouldn't be very pleased with you, I expect?'

'Actually, they were awfully decent about it. But — well, it's the second time I've boobed, at least, that's what they'll be thinking. Yesterday, when a man was shot at in one of the caravans over yonder' — he waved a hand — 'one of the women, she's the wife of the man who was shot — she said they'd given this man a lift and he'd got out of the car at the site gates. Well, that wasn't true. I was in the snack bar across there for ages and I didn't see a single person get out of a car there. I told the police but they didn't seem to believe me.' He leaned forward. 'It's my belief the people in those two vans are up to something queer, and I mean to find out what it is, so I'm keeping an eye on them.'

'That could get you into trouble, though,' Molly said. 'I wouldn't take too many risks if I were you . . . Those C.I.D men you were with, I recognised one of them. Inspector Dykes. I'm staying at the Burleigh Hotel, where a robbery took place last night, and he was questioning us all early this morning. He hadn't the other with him then, though.'

'You mean Sergeant Garrett? Well, you see, he's not on the Whitsea force. He's on sick leave here and just sort of helping.'

Molly got up. 'I must be going. Thanks so very much for the tea, Colin, dear, and for finding my brooch.'

'Glad I did, Miss Brown — Molly, I

mean. I'll walk as far as the gates with you.'

'No, I've put you to enough trouble. Be seeing you again sometime!' And she was gone before Colin could say another word.

She hurried to the main road, saw the telephone kiosk on the far side, crossed to it and picked up the local directory. She found a number and dialled.

'Macey's Taxi Service, Esplanade Rank,' a voice answered.

Molly put in her sixpence. 'I want a taxi to take me to Healthways Guest House,' she said. 'I'm in Northway Road opposite the municipal caravan site. The cab can pick me up there — I'll be looking out for it.'

'Be with you in a couple of minutes, madam,' the voice promised.

9

Molly Bilton was not a woman who made snap decisions unless an instinct, one which from experience she had come to trust, dictated them. As 'Molly Brown' to him, she had listened very carefully to Colin Taylor's account of his two visits to Healthways. The odd questions she had flung in here and there during that account had convinced her the boy really had seen Ray Lever at the guest house, and when, at her insistence, he had described Pelford, the proprietor, a bell had rung very loudly in her mind.

Molly's father, Jack Bilton, had been a professional criminal by choice. In the line of organised robbery, he had looked upon crime as his vocation. He had been moderately successful at it. Working with a small gang of hand-picked associates, he had achieved a number of solid though unspectacular coups, he had lived quietly and his wife and only daughter were well provided for. On two occasions his plans had gone awry, on each of them he took the rap personally, keeping his confederates out of trouble and 'doing his bird' quite cheerfully.

Molly was twenty-four, and working at a dull office job, when her mother was stricken with cancer. His wife's death broke Jack Bilton up completely. Six months later, his car, apparently out of control, crashed into a concrete bridge one winter's night. He was killed instantly, and in her own mind Molly was certain the accident had been self-induced.

Latterly, partly because she had become tired of a life ruled by routine, partly because she and her father had always been very close, she had begun to work alongside him in his illegal ventures. It seemed the natural thing, both to herself and to her father's partners, that, at his death, she should take over his role. The Kendalls, the Reads and the rest of them had had no complaints of her leadership. Well, not until now, she reflected, as she stepped into the taxi. She had sensed their feeling that she had made an error in bringing in a man like Lever, and this was a matter she must put right at once.

Pelford . . . Martin Pelford . . . Her father had mentioned the name, that of a man he had met in Strangeways during his last residence there. He'd described him to Molly, too. She was certain he was the man she hoped to meet in a very few minutes.

She paid off the taxi at the front door of the guest house and stood there watching until the driver had negotiated his return to the road. When she turned towards the house the front door had been opened. A dark-haired, sleek-looking young woman in a white overall coat was standing on the steps. She smiled formally at Molly.

'Good afternoon, madam. Can I help you?'

'Yes.' Molly spoke crisply. 'I'd like to see Mr. Pelford. Is he at home?'

'He is, but if it's a question of accommodation, that's my department. If you care to step in, please . . . ' She stood aside invitingly.

Molly went past her into the hall.

'This is merely a personal visit,' she said over her shoulder. 'Would you tell Mr. Pelford the daughter of an old friend of his, Jack Bilton, would like to speak to him?'

'Of course.' But the girl made no move to carry out the visitor's request. She looked keenly at Molly.

'Excuse me, but what was the name again?'

'Bilton. Not too difficult to remember, surely?'

A flush of annoyance flooded the girl's tanned face.

'You seem to be quite sure you'll get to see him,' she returned sharply. 'I mean, sending your taxi away, and that.'

'I usually get what I want,' Molly told her. 'So, if it isn't asking too much of you . . .'

The girl flounced away without another word and Molly, who hadn't been offered a chair, took one which seemed fairly comfortable and sank into it, looking about her with considerable interest. If this was the background to a crook set-up, Pelford, at its head, must have money behind him somewhere; on the other hand, she could be entirely wrong about him and this was another Pelford, strictly legit. It was a point she was determined to settle.

A rosy-faced man with heavy spectacles came into the hall, smiling amicably.

'This is indeed a pleasure! My receptionist tells me you are Jack Bilton's daughter.'

Molly stood up. She had planned a direct attack, which she expected would have been met by evasions, denials, and outright lies. The man's approach rather took the wind out of her sails.

'Yes. Molly Bilton. My father knew you — '

'In Strangeways.' Pelford raised his hands in a self-deprecatory gesture. 'It must be all of six years ago. But please do come into my office, Miss Bilton. I'm sure we have lots to talk about.'

He seated her in a chair and faced her across his desk, he offered her a drink, which Molly refused. Then he clasped his hands on the desk top, apparently completely relaxed and ready for a long chat.

'And how is your father?' he began.

'He died nearly two years ago,' Molly returned. She was back on her normal keel now, watchful, coolly calculating.

'Really?' Pelford jerked upright. 'I'm terribly sorry — I had no idea! You see,' he went on, 'though my term in Strangeways wasn't the first I'd served, it taught me the ultimate lesson. The life I'd been living was just not worthwhile. When I came out, I went straight.'

'You seem to have done very well for yourself, too.' Molly waved a slim hand around.

'Well, Miss Bilton, with all due modesty, I can claim to be not without brains. I had a little money saved and when I decided to break with the old ways, I made a few profitable investments and so — here I am.'

Molly leaned forward. 'One of the investments being that wages snatch at Rochester, followed by the Brighton hotel clean-out. My father, you know, kept tabs on all his former — er — professional friends and I remember him telling me those two jobs had your signature all over them.'

Pelford smiled patiently. 'Your father was completely mistaken, Miss Bilton. Much as you may despise me for it, I am now a law-abiding citizen. My interests have led me to buy and run this guest house for the benefit of people seeking health in pleasant surroundings — '

Molly cut in sharply. 'Are you making money out of it?'

'That is an impertinent question. However, I will answer it. This is our first full season here. We need time to build up a connection. I do not expect — I never did — to make a profit this year.'

'Fair enough. And it wouldn't help that connection-building if the jacks knew an ex-con was running this place, would it? They may not have anything on you here — not yet, at any rate — but they'd keep a very watchful eye on you. And you might find that extremely embarrassing, Mr. Martin Pelford.'

He took off his spectacles, opened a

drawer in his desk, and after some fumbling therein, produced a small square of chamois leather. He began to polish the spectacles, looking at her with knitted brows as his fingers moved gently over the glass.

'What exactly is the object of your visit here, Miss Bilton?'

'A double-barrelled one. First, I think — I'm sure — you have a man in my employ hiding up here, a man called Raymond Lever. I want him back. Second, I've every good reason to suspect who's behind the hotel jobs, and the others, which have been pulled in Whitsea recently. In a word — you.' She was smiling now, watching him closely, certain from the swift expression she had seen in his unguarded eyes that her intuitions were sound.

'Look,' she said persuasively, 'dog doesn't eat dog. You can't go on operating here so easily while I and my people are around, and we're at Whitsea for pickings, too, So what about a temporary merger?'

Pelford replaced his glasses. 'Obviously, you have some terms in mind.'

'Sure thing. I get Lever back, we table any plans each of us has so that we don't get in each other's way — in fact, we'll probably be able to help each other. There's room for both of us here, you know.'

Pelford picked up the piece of chamois leather and returned it to the desk drawer. He closed the drawer and pushed his chair back, rising to his feet.

'I know nothing about this man Lever, I am in legitimate business here and I intend to stay that way. We have nothing more to say to each other, I think, Miss Bilton. May I have the pleasure of seeing you out?'

Molly made no attempt to move. 'I meant what I said just now, you know, about getting a whisper to the cops that Martin Pelford, ex-con, is in their midst. They already suspect Lever is on these premises. You won't find life very happy if they really start bearing down on you.'

'I see. In that case . . . ' He reached out to press a bell-stud on the desk. Almost at once the door opened and the reception-ist came in. Pelford said, 'Ah, Miss

Henson. Just a moment.' For the second time he opened the desk drawer, but now he took from it a small, neat case. 'Would you be good enough to put this tape recorder in a place of safety?'

The girl said, 'Yes, Mr. Pelford,' took the case and went out. Pelford smiled gently.

'I switched it on at the point where I asked what your object was in coming here, Miss Bilton. I think you will agree that your subsequent remarks tell exactly why you are in Whitsea. If I hear any more from you, that tape goes to the police.' His voice hardened. He strode across to the door. 'I'm giving you a chance because I knew your father. Otherwise, I should inform on you at once. And now get out of here — quick!'

Set-faced, Molly walked past him, out of the front door, down the drive. From his office window Pelford watched her and now his eyes were hard behind his spectacles, his grin maliciously triumphant.

10

Detective Inspector Spratt, seated at a desk in the small office Superintendent Welling had put at his disposal at Whitsea Central, called, 'Come in!' He grinned an immediate welcome when Garrett opened the door and entered.

'Ah, Dick!' he greeted. 'And how's your health and temper on this fine Monday morning?'

'No complaints, sir, thanks.' Garrett stood, hesitant, just inside the room. 'I happened to be passing and I thought you wouldn't mind if I just called in for a minute or so.'

'Glad to see you, lad. Pull up a chair.' Spratt shuffled papers into a loose pile and pushed them aside. He jerked a thumb at the pile.

'I've been working on the hotel jobs — spent the weekend studying and analysing reports, trying to find some definite picture, but there just isn't one as

151

far as I can see. You can test Welling's theory of two gangs at work here, or try Dykes' suggestion of a single gang only — and get nowhere with either of them.'

He picked up a folder and flicked through its contents.

'The locals got in touch with Theaker, the man with the lady friend, who was shot at on the cliffs. He admitted, after a little pressure, that he was the chap concerned but he couldn't tell them any more than he told you. The Palladium box-office hold-up is still wrapped in deepest mystery, too.'

'Anything more on the whisper about a forthcoming bank robbery, sir?'

'None at all. That could be a real red herring. You know as well as I do how these narks'll dream up a so-called piece of information when they're short of a few bob and know an officer who'll oblige. And yet you can't turn 'em down altogether. You never know when they'll come through with a slice of the real stuff.'

Spratt's glance strayed to his watch and Garrett got up promptly

'I mustn't waste your time, sir. Only, naturally, I was interested. And if there's anything I can do at all, I'll be only too glad.'

'I'll bear it in mind, depend on that,' Spratt replied. 'Meanwhile, you make the most of this weather while it lasts. And drop in again, anytime you like, Dick.'

Garrett walked back across the town towards Cliffside. He didn't feel like making the journey down to the sands. He'd already done the up-the-coast-and-back trip on the 'Whitsea Queen,' and he was getting tired of sitting in parks staring at flower beds.

He grinned suddenly, realising all these points merely added up to an excuse for visiting the caravan site again. It had become, for him, the main centre of interest in Whitsea, he was certain there was something odd going on there, and though it wasn't his business to poke his nose into the province of the local C.I.D., there could be no harm in taking another look round. He might even find the opportunity of more talk with Colin

Taylor. That young man needed watching, he fancied himself, Garrett thought, as a bit of a private eye. Which could be dangerous.

Garrett walked on to the site, and noted a cream-coloured Super Minx, with a Deniston registration, which was parked just inside the entrance. He passed the two vans in which he was interested. A man with a strip of plaster on his neck was standing in the doorway of the Kendalls' van. That would be Kendall himself, Garrett decided. He hadn't seen the chap until now.

Near the far end of the site he found Colin, on a makeshift cricket pitch, facing the bowling of a younger boy, while a fair-haired man kept wicket and a smiling woman stood, as fielder, on the leg side.

Colin hit the ball back to Keith Jackson. He looked up.

'Mr. Garrett!' He waved his bat. 'Come and join in! Meet Mr. and Mrs. Jackson and Keith. Mr. Garrett's a friend of mine and he's a C.I.D. man,' he told the others, with some pride.

'Sorry,' Garrett said, 'but I'm afraid my

leg won't stand cricket yet.' It was clear he wouldn't be able to get Colin on his own for some time, and he didn't want to make an issue of what had been merely an impulse. 'I was passing by and I thought I'd come across and say hello,' he added.

'Glad you did, Mr. Garrett.' Colin's head jerked up as he looked beyond the sergeant. 'And what d'you know! Here's Miss Brown, too! I told you, Keith, didn't I, how I found a brooch for her yesterday?'

Garrett watched the tall chestnut-haired young woman who approached them. She was smiling somewhat diffidently, as if she weren't sure if an intrusion on the party would be welcome.

'I thought I really must come and say thank you again, Colin,' she said in a rich contralto voice. 'You can't think how much I value that brooch.' She addressed Mrs. Jackson. 'It was my mother's, you see. She gave it to me just before she died.'

Garrett said, 'Well, I'll be getting on,' and turned away. Colin seemed all right this morning, more normal, his former boredom gone. If the Jacksons were taking him up, he'd probably forget his sleuthing interests. No need to have further qualms about the lad.

He was almost at the site gates again when a voice said huskily, 'Oh, excuse me!' and there was the chestnut-haired Miss Brown hurrying across the grass. Garrett stopped, looked enquiringly at her.

'I'm so sorry to bother you.' She sounded nervous, a little upset. 'But I have a problem, and I understand from Colin Taylor you are a policeman — a detective.'

'That's my job — er — Miss Brown, isn't it? But I'm on sick leave here, I'm not attached to the local force. So if you have any troubles, you must speak to a Whitsea officer.'

She twisted slim fingers together. 'That's just the snag, you see. I have to keep it unofficial for the moment. It's advice I want, only that. Look, Mr. Garrett — Colin gave me your name — could you spare me just a few minutes?

There's the snack bar across the road. May I tell you all about it over a cup of coffee?'

Garrett was only human — and he was on holiday, with time on his hands. In those circumstances, he reacted as any red-blooded male does when a lovely girl appeals to him.

'Okay,' he said. 'Let's go.'

The snack bar was not particularly full, Garrett pointed to a table in one corner and went to the counter. He bought coffee and chocolate biscuits and carried them across to his companion. She thanked him very prettily when he handed her a cup, but shook her head as he sat down and pushed the biscuits towards her.

'I love them,' she said, 'but I have to watch my figure, you know.' She seemed to have lost her former trace of nervousness. Garrett reached for a biscuit and began to unwrap it.

'Well, Miss Brown, what is this little problem that's worrying you?'

She stirred her coffee, looking levelly at him.

'First of all, Mr. Garrett, let's get the record straight. My name is Bilton, Molly Bilton. Colin Taylor, I think, misheard me when I introduced myself to him yesterday. I didn't correct him this morning because I thought he'd feel a little embarrassed, having made a mistake, and he and I aren't likely to meet again. So you've got that, have you? Molly Bilton.'

The emphasis she put on the surname, and the way she was looking at him, puzzled Garrett.

'Yes, I've got it,' he said, 'but should I recognise the name? You said it as if I ought to. Am I talking to a celebrity of some sort?'

She replied with a question of her own.

'Where are you stationed when you are on duty?'

'Deniston. I work with the Regional Crime Squad there.'

'In that case, you should recognise — But wait a moment. You probably wouldn't know my father when he — er — worked from there. You're too young.'

'And still puzzled, Miss Bilton.'

158

'Oh, do call me Molly. I hate the formalities.' She took the spoon out of her cup, laid it in the saucer and raised the cup to her lips, looking at him over the rim. 'My father was a man with form, a crook, a villain, one of the baddies, an ex-con — you can use what label you like.'

She took a tiny sip of coffee and put the cup down with a hand which was perfectly steady.

'We can't all be on the side of the law,' Garrett said casually, 'or what would coppers do for a living? You said your father was one of our clients. Past tense.'

'He died some two years ago. Car crash.'

'I'm sorry.' Garrett left it at that. It was up to her to carry on.

'If you look at the records,' she continued, 'you'll find he served several stretches in prison. One of these was at Strangeways. Now, look, Mr. Garrett. My father never tried to hide what he did for a living from my mother — she's dead, too — or from myself. After I grew up, that is. Crime was his profession, and he

159

was more than good at it. Your people caught him once or twice, but you can't win all the time, and it wasn't always his fault he got fingered. People — his associates — let him down.'

Like most policemen, Garrett had a sneaking feeling of admiration for the professional crook, who is quite open, when he has to be, about his activities, who is proud of his knowledge and skills, and who usually takes his medicine cheerfully enough. Inside prison walls these men are seldom trouble-makers, though they know their rights and see to it that they get them. Maximum remission is their object inside, outside once more they take up the game where they left it off, like chess players after an interruption. Across the board from them, the police seek another checkmate, hoping, like their opponents, that the luck of the game may be theirs this time.

So Garrett, drinking coffee with a crook's daughter who certainly wasn't ashamed of her ancestry, was neither shocked nor disturbed by her revelation. But his casual manner now had an inner backing of professional wariness.

'We still haven't got to your problem yet, have we?'

She seemed to relax, as if she were glad the preliminary explanations were done with.

'Coming right up, sir,' she said with a smile, and then, at once, was serious again.

'The Whitsea police are looking for a man who did some shooting at the caravan site across the way — right?'

Garrett nodded. 'Well?'

'I think — I'm sure — I saw him yesterday evening.' She held up a hand as Garrett drew breath to speak. 'No. Don't tell me I should have reported this to the police at once. Wait till you've heard the whole story.

'My car has been in dock since I arrived here last Friday — brake trouble which developed on the journey. I collected it from the garage on Saturday evening. Yesterday, after dinner, about eight o'clock, I took it out for a run, turned off Northway Road and did a sort of circular tour.

'I was driving along a road and was approaching a biggish house with a wall bordering the road. A man came out of a side gate and waited until I'd passed before he crossed the road. As I was drawing level with him he turned his back on me. I felt sure I ought to know who he was, as if I'd seen him before somewhere. The answer hit me about half a mile further on. He measured up to the description of the wanted gunman. I'd read this in the local press on Saturday evening.

'I reversed the car and drove back, wanting a second look at him, if possible, to make sure. But he was no longer there. I pulled up, got out of the car and walked to the main gates of this place. There was a board which said 'Healthways Guest House.''

Garrett kept his face poker-straight. 'Don't forget your coffee,' he said. 'It'll be getting cold.'

Molly nodded and took a long drink. 'You *are* interested, aren't you?' she said as she put the cup down.

'Of course. I'm still waiting for the

problem, though.'

'Right. This board gave the proprietor's name as M. Pelford. Which rang a bell. My father had met a Martin Pelford in Strangeways, and Pelford isn't a common name. This guest house proprietor could be the same man. Now you see my difficulty. If the wanted bloke — the gunman — was hiding up there, and I reported it, Martin Pelford would be in trouble — from me. Putting my father's friends in bad isn't the sort of thing I care to do. And yet . . . Well I'll be honest with you, Mr. Garrett. If this man on the run had knocked off a bank, or anything like that, I'd have kept quiet about seeing him. But a gunman, and by all accounts half-crazy, running around loose, that's a different matter. Yet, as I say, I didn't want to get Martin Pelford into trouble. That was the problem.

'I thought about it all last night and this morning. When I learnt you were a policeman I thought you might be able to help. Is there any way I can report seeing this man without Martin Pelford knowing who it was who put the scuffers — sorry, the police — on to him?'

'That's easy enough,' Garrett returned. 'I happen to know the inspector in charge of that shooting job. I'll pass on what you've told me without mentioning your name. The old 'information received' stunt, you know. If he decides to investigate this guest house, and finds his man there, he won't worry where the whisper came from. You just leave it to me.'

Molly let out a long sigh of relief.

'That certainly eases my mind. Dad may not have been always on the side of the law, but he was dead against violence, and shooting, and he brought me up in the same frame of mind.' She finished her coffee. 'You don't happen to know, I suppose, if the local people have anything on Martin Pelford already?'

'I haven't the faintest.' Garrett also drained his cup. 'Where have you been staying in Whitsea?'

'The Burleigh Hotel. But — Look here, you don't mean — I wouldn't be expected to identify this gunman, or be brought into the job in any way? I mean, this is all unofficial, between you and me. I've told you, and now I don't want to have any more to do with it.' She pushed back her chair and got up hurriedly.

'Not to worry,' Garrett assured her. 'Unofficial's the word. I'll give Inspector Dykes a ring and that'll be the end of it as far as you're concerned.' He looked at his watch. 'I'll do it now, from my boarding house.'

He followed Molly out, wished her good-bye. Without a backward look he walked towards Cliffside, but he stopped at a little shop some short distance away, where a stand of picture postcards, outside the shop, gave him adequate cover. From here he saw Molly Bilton return to the caravan site, and, less than a minute later, she drove out in the cream-coloured Super Minx he had seen parked there. She turned towards the town centre, but drew into the kerb and stopped some hundred yards from the site gates. Garrett went on slowly rotating the cards on their stand, he saw a sharp-faced woman in the shop was keeping an eye on him, but he didn't want to move yet. A thrill of satisfaction went through him when he spotted Dennis Read come from the site and walk down the road towards the Super Minx.

He opened the door of the car and got inside, sitting next to the driver. The two began a conversation, Garrett could see their heads leaning towards each other, through the car's rear window. He took a postcard out of the stand, glanced at it, put it back and chose another.

The conversation did not last long. Read got out of the car, went back to the caravan site. Garrett entered the shop and paid for his card before walking on to Cliffside.

11

'So this Molly Bilton tells me a long and involved story about Martin Pelford,' Garrett summarised, 'and then she and Read have a get-together. Bilton's car was parked by Read's caravan on the site. It all makes you think.'

It was early afternoon and he was sitting in Inspector Dykes' office, with Spratt holding a watching brief at his side. Dykes looked up from the notes he had been scribbling.

'This woman was a guest at the Burleigh Hotel when it was done over. But that might be pure coincidence. We've never heard of her before in these parts. You say her car has a Deniston registration, though. What about it, Mr. Spratt?'

'I knew her father, Jack Bilton,' Spratt replied. 'In fact, I put him inside for one of his stretches. I'd just been made sergeant at the time and I was rather proud of myself, I remember. Jack was living in Deniston at the time, then he went to Manchester and we heard of him later in — let's see — Leicester, I think. He came back to Deniston when his wife fell ill; I remember meeting him and he told me about her trouble. Jack was never a man to bear a grudge. He thought she'd get the best medical attention in Deniston. He said he'd packed in the old life, but that's a yarn you often hear from an ex-con. Odd, though, that his daughter should turn up here. She's no form, as far as I know.'

'But you, sergeant,' Dykes said, 'got the impression she told you she'd seen that gunman bloke near Healthways to put us on Pelford's track, in spite of what she actually said to you? Also, it's clear she's pretty friendly with the Kendalls and the Reads.'

'Pelford's an old lag,' Spratt said. 'If he is the same man Jack Bilton knew. Anyway, we have a Pelford in Whitsea, running an off-beat guest house. We also have — or had, if I may be optimistic — a series of nicely-pulled jobs in Whitsea.

Those are my pigeon, so you can leave Pelford to me and I'll see what I can dig up from Regional H.Q. and from the C.R.O. Meanwhile, we have Molly Bilton, freely admitting her crook ancestry, for some reason best known to herself.

'If you'll take my advice, inspector, I'd start bearing down a bit on those two caravan families. Find their exact connection with Molly. If you can spare a man to keep a general eye on that site, so much the better.'

'That's just the trouble.' Dykes put a mournful note into his voice. 'I'm short-staffed to the limit.' He kept his eyes from Garrett's face.

Garrett said casually, 'Of course, as I've told Mr. Spratt, if there's anything I can do . . . '

'I'd be most grateful if you would help,' Dykes said quickly. 'I don't mean anything very concentrated or prolonged. Just sort of keeping an eye lifting anytime you're around there.' He glanced at his watch. 'As you say, Mr. Spratt, the Reads and the Kendalls could do with another chat-up. I'll slip across there this

169

afternoon — Yes? Come in!'

Detective Sergeant Prior, the plump red-haired young man whom Garrett had met at Superintendent Welling's conference the previous morning, entered the room.

'Excuse me,' he said, and looked at Dykes. 'Mr, Welling, sir. He's just been on at me about Puffer Tenby and I wondered if . . . Well, sir, I could do with a bit of help, and the Super said if I got in touch with Sergeant Garrett, he might . . . You see, sir, I want Puffer watched, and he knows all of us in the Whitsea force.'

Spratt grinned at Garrett. 'You made a big mistake, you know, getting into this in the first place. There you were, a free man on holiday, with not a care in the world, and now look!'

'Think about it, sergeant,' Dykes advised. 'We don't want to twist your arm, you know.'

'That's all right, sir. Glad to do what I can.'

'Then if you'd like to go with Prior, and see what he wants — only, don't forget, I've first call on you for that site offer.'

The two sergeants went out together. Dykes said, 'We're not pushing him too much, I hope, sir?'

'No danger of that with Garrett,' Spratt returned. 'He'll do you a good job, but at his own pace, while he's on convalescent leave. He won't take undue risks, he's too keen to get back to his own work in Deniston.'

'Fair enough, sir. Now, before I go out to that site, I'd just like to get my mind clear on this Molly Bilton. D'you think there's any chance she's following in father's footsteps?'

'Possible, I suppose. I don't know her, you see. We could get some background, of course. One thing's certain in my opinion, she can't be behind these jobs here I'm working on. True, she's staying at the Burleigh, but, like the rest of the guests there, she was cleared of any suspicion of collusion, and when she tells Garrett she arrived in Whitsea on Friday last, I'm inclined to believe it. I don't think she had anything to do with the said jobs. They were done before she got here.'

'Except for the box-office hold-up,' Dykes reminded him. 'And if she organised that on the spur, she's a real star performer. The sort I just hate to have on my patch.'

Spratt went back to his own room, opened a file which lay on his desk and called the switchboard. He asked for the direct line to Regional C.I.D. at Deniston. Seventy miles away, the desk clerk acknowledged his call.

'Inspector Spratt here, Is Mr. Hallam around?'

'He's in his office, sir, shall I connect you?'

Spratt grunted, 'Please,' and then the Chief Superintendent's voice came over.

'That you, Jack? Fire away.'

'Up to now, sir, all the cartridges have been blanks, I'm ringing for information. Molly Bilton, old Jack's daughter, has turned up here and it's just possible she may be involved. She gave her address' — he ran a finger down a list on the file which carried the details of the Burleigh Hotel guests — 'as 16 Holroyd Avenue,

Deniston 12. I'd like that checked, and also details of her present job, if any, background, all that. I don't want to grill her myself at the moment.'

'I'll have it seen to at once,' Hallam promised.

'Next, Martin Pelford. Alleged to have form, at present running a guest house called Healthways here. Did at least one stretch in Strangeways — don't know how long ago. Anything on him would be gratefully received. There's also . . . ' He paused, thinking of the Reads and the Kendalls. 'But never mind that for the moment, sir. Just some people I'll have looked up here, possibly. That's about all for now.'

'Your gang or gangs seem to be taking a few days off, Jack. Or has something broken I haven't heard about yet?'

'All quiet at the moment, sir. That goes for me, too, I'm sorry to say. Not a single lead anywhere.'

'You'll find one, Jack. I'll ring you back at the earliest.'

Spratt put the telephone down, wishing he could share Hallam's confidence. He began to think about Martin Pelford, the proprietor of the Healthways Guest House, the only name in his Whitsea file which had a police record attached to it.

He got up and crossed to the window. Below him, in the streets, the life of a popular seaside resort at the height of its season flowed to and fro. Beyond, in a gap between buildings, he caught a glimpse of the sun-shimmering sea. For almost forty-eight hours his mind had been bent to the task he had been given; he had studied reports, sifted evidence, moved the jig-saw pieces here and there, trying to find the start of a pattern on which he could build. But he hadn't been able to fit even two of those pieces together.

He stretched limbs and muscles wearied by sitting at a desk, longing for action. A trip to this Healthways place, and a few words with its proprietor? It was tempting, yet he didn't wish to put a possible suspect on his guard — yet.

He turned away from the window and slumped glumly into his chair again. There was a rattle of crockery outside, and a knock at the door. The young constable, Liversidge, who had served coffee at the previous day's conference, came in with a tea-tray.

'Thought you might like a cup, sir. It's a dry sort of afternoon.'

'You couldn't have had a better thought, lad! I'm just about dying for a swallow.'

The tea, sweet and strong, as he liked it, restored Spratt's mental energy, and his optimism. When you're stuck, start over again from the beginning. This had always been one of his firmly-held tenets. He proceeded to apply it.

Half an hour later his telephone rang. He picked up the receiver and found Hallam on the line.

'I've been pushing things around for you, Jack. First, Molly Bilton. She's been living at the address she gave for eight months. She's rooming there with a widow. Mrs. Whitburn says she's an excellent lodger, quote, a lovely young woman, unquote. Seems to be comfortably off, runs a car and claims to be a free-lance journalist. This means irregular hours. Staying at Whitsea for several weeks, Mrs. Whitburn to be notified of her return. Went there on Friday. Never brings friends to the house, receives a normal amount of correspondence. Not much there for you, I'm afraid, but we'll keep digging on your say-so.

'Martin Pelford. Two convictions for robbery, one from a Leicester hotel, one from a big store in the same city. Does that make you prick up your ears? In both cases the jobs were carefully organised, Pelford apparently being the boss of a little group of villains, all of whom were taken with him on the second job. Nothing known against him for the past four years. He left Leicester, present address unknown. The Leicester police are putting details of both jobs he did there, M.O. and the lot, on the teleprinter, so you should get it anytime now. The stuff he netted from the second job, mainly furs and jewellery, weren't recovered, so he could have had capital to set up some sort of business when the heat was off. On his first conviction he worked with a youngish fellow called

Canwell who had a reputation for strong-arm stuff. And that's the lot for now.'

'Thanks again, sir.' Spratt dropped the pencil he had been using to scribble notes. 'Re Molly Bilton. I'll let you know if I need anything else on her. We can lay her off for the moment.'

'Right. Well, don't overdo the sunbathing, Jack.'

'That'll be the day, sir,' Spratt responded, and, still hoping for the best, went down to the main office to consult the teleprinter.

12

For once, that Monday evening, Mrs. Taylor had bestirred herself and had prepared an evening meal in the caravan, to which her son Colin brought a healthy adolescent appetite.

As he helped to wash up, he said, 'There's a big firework display in Royal Park tonight, mum. What say we all go to it?'

His mother's eyes slid guiltily away from his eager face.

'That would be lovely, darling, only . . . Well, you see, daddy and I met some really wonderful people on the course this afternoon, and we all arranged to meet this evening for a drink and a chat. But you go to the display, Colin. I'm sure you'll love it. Have you plenty of money?'

Colin nodded. It was no use arguing. And having seen them off, he walked slowly across the site, glancing at the two caravans which specially interested him.

They seemed to be totally deserted.

He went on into the town, not caring much if he saw the mouldy fireworks or not. It was too early for them yet, anyway. On the foreshore near the harbour were several amusement arcades, and, to put time on, he had visited them frequently of late. He turned into the nearest, obtained change for a shilling and bet himself he could make that amount of copper spin out at least a quarter of an hour. He lost his bet by four minutes.

There was an area of ground alongside the entrance to the harbour basin where a fun fair was now in full swing. Colin wandered around it, had one go on the helter-skelter, two on the dodgem cars, several at the shooting gallery. Dusk was deepening into darkness when he turned his back on the garishly-lit fair and faced the steep road back to the site. The sense of utter boredom which he had experienced so often in the past week clamped down on him again. There was just nothing to do but to go back to the caravan — for he had given up the idea of the fireworks — and wait there until his parents returned. Then supper and bed.

Lights were shining behind the drawn curtains of most of the caravans when he reached the site. The Reads' van was in darkness, but the Kendalls' was lit up. He went quietly across the grass towards it.

There seemed to be something going on inside, he could distinguish several voices. The door was closed but one of the curtained side windows was partly open. Colin's boredom disappeared as he moved cautiously nearer. He peered carefully around, satisfying himself no-one was watching him. He squatted beneath the window so that his head wouldn't show up against the light. Almost at once his attention was held by Mrs. Read's voice.

'It's all very well for Molly to give her orders,' she was saying, and her tone was querulous. 'She's all right, doing the large in a posh hotel while we pig it here. And she doesn't have to take any of the risks, either.'

Her husband's voice answered her.

'Look, love, we've got to make certain, haven't we? Or as certain as we can. If he's there, we can bet he's blown on us by now, and this bloke Pelford can just walk in and take the pickings, after all the trouble we've had setting the job up. If he's not at this Healthways spot, we know we can go ahead. It's as clear cut as that. Don't you agree, Dulcie?'

'I agree it's worth a try,' Mrs. Kendall returned. 'Though, let's face it, you're taking on long odds. If he is there, he'll be kept well and truly out of sight. At the same time, nothing venture, nothing win. You just may be lucky, Dennis. Let's hope you are. Watch it you don't get caught, though.'

'That doesn't worry me. If I am spotted around the place, Pelford's reaction'll be that I'm a plain clothes cop, you can bet.'

'I wonder if he really is on the square these days?' That was Mrs. Kendall's voice. Read chuckled in reply.

'Can a leopard change its spots? No, I'm pretty sure Molly's theory is the right one. Look, if I'm going I'd better be making a move soon.'

'You've time for another cup of coffee.'

'Well, just a quick one, Dulcie.'

Colin moved away from the caravan. The idea which had entered his mind had set his heart thumping with excitement. Mr. Read was proposing to pay a secret visit to Healthways. He was hoping to find something — or somebody. And he, Colin, wanted to be there, too.

He was out of the site and walking fast up Northway Road before he had definitely made up his mind to go through with this thing.

Healthways was just over a mile away. He could do it in a quarter of an hour, easily. Read, of course, would use his car, but Colin felt he had at least five minutes start on him. With his long legs covering the ground at a spanking pace, and suppressing a desire to break into a run, Colin kept to the left-hand side of the road. He had memorised the number of the Triumph Herald and after a few minutes walking he began to keep an eye on the rear plates of the cars which passed him.

Panting a little, he was in sight of the side road which led to Healthways when the Herald passed him. The risk that

Read would notice him going in the same direction was, Colin thought, not a great one. In any case, it had to be taken.

He saw Read's brake lights come on as the car slowed for the left-hand turn and disappeared. Colin reduced his own pace. The side road would not be brilliantly lit, he knew. Read would likely park some little distance from the guest house, might even sit in his car for a while, working out his next move. Colin didn't want to be seen; he reached the turn and went cautiously round it. There were a number of cars under the lamps which served the housing site beyond which Healthways was situated. Colin approached each car with care, but none of them was occupied. He found the Triumph Herald with its side lights on, level with the last of the houses. Ahead, some hundred yards away, he saw Read walking quickly forward. Colin shrank back into the shadows until his man had turned a bend in the road.

He went forward, eyes and ears alert. When he had passed the bend Read wasn't in sight. Colin pulled up and caught the click of iron on iron from the other side of the road, ahead. That was where the drive gates of Healthways were situated.

Entirely consumed now by the thrills of the chase, the boy went on, still keeping to the left-hand side of the road. The drive gates were slightly open when he came opposite to them. He couldn't see Read at all, but he knew the man must have gone through the gates. Colin stepped back into a patch of shadow. He didn't intend to blunder into the guest house premises until he could be certain Read was out of the way. He caught a movement under a tree just inside the grounds, and Read came out into the light cast by the street lamps. He had obviously been surveying Healthways. So that proved he wasn't there for any normal, legitimate reason. As an ordinary visitor, he would have walked up the drive to the front door.

Colin moved to one side, centring Read in his field of vision. The man began to walk across the lawn, diagonally, aiming for the rear premises of the house. Colin crossed the road and made a careful survey through the gates. Read was a fair distance from him now, he judged it safe to slip sideways through the gap between the two gates and to take up a position under the tree Read had used.

From here he saw his man going along the path which led to the back of the house. Colin noted that two of the windows facing the drive were lighted, he could just make out the heads and shoulders of several people, all staring in one direction, at a T.V. set, he guessed. The rest of the house facing him was in complete darkness.

Well, he hadn't come all this way just to stand staring at the front of a house. He wanted to know what Read was up to, and to find the answer to this problem he must follow him. There was quite a risk that Read might reappear, going back to his car, and might spot his follower. That risk had to be taken. Colin was sure he could give a good account of himself, in the business of dodging out of the way, if matters came to that. There was always a line of retreat open to him through the shrubbery and over the wall. Quite confidently, he left the cover of the tree and hurried forward on the course Read had taken.

When he stepped off the grass of the lawn on to the path, he saw this was made up of crazy paving on which his rubber-soled shoes would make no sound. He turned the angle of the house and came upon a high stone wall, with a wide archway in its centre which seemed to give entrance to some sort of rear court. He slid round the side of the arch, keeping in a pool of shadow. Now he saw he was in a back yard, a spacious area of concrete.

Facing him was a rear wing of the house, now completely dark. On his left he could see what seemed to be an open-fronted shed — a second look identified it as a garage with a car inside. On his right was the back door of the house with a lighted window at one side of it. This was some eight feet up in the wall, and Colin now saw that to Read it was a centre of great interest. The man was standing on a lidded dustbin, set beneath the window. He was peering in at one side, his left hand spread out against the wall, the fingers of his right clutching the windowsill.

So he came here to do a little spying, Colin thought, and recalled the conversation he had heard from inside the Kendalls' caravan. Read was trying to find out if a certain 'he' was here at Healthways. And since these were the back premises, 'he' wouldn't be one of the paying guests. Colin had a very good idea who 'he' was by now. He strained his ears to listen and could hear someone talking behind that lit window and the sound was becoming louder, as if someone had moved nearer to the window.

Read pulled his head quickly back, but remained standing on the bin. Any moment now, Colin thought, he's going to get down and beat it back to his car. In which case, it'll be safer for me to be behind him, out of sight. He moved quietly sideways along the wall, in the direction of the open garage.

Read left his post very suddenly, very unexpectedly. The lid slipped sideways off the dustbin beneath his feet. It fell on to the concrete with a deafening clatter, Read staggered, but managed to keep his balance. As he darted for safety through the archway the back door was wrenched open. The wedge of brilliance which shot from the brightly-lit passage behind it caught Colin fair and square, like a lime picking out an actor on a dark stage. He shrank back against the wall, momentarily dazzled.

A big man leapt from behind the door into the yard as if he were aiming at an Olympic long-jump record.

Without uttering a sound, he dived for Colin with outspread arms, curled fingers ready to clutch. Colin didn't wait for his arrival. This was only a Rugby full back, menacing a stand-off half sprinting for the try line, and Colin had faced quite a few of those in his time. He sprang off his toes and hurtled forward to meet the oncoming man. At the last split second he would do one of his lightning swerves, ducking under those arms and going fast for the archway exit. It might have come off on a football pitch. No large patch of engine oil there to set him skidding, pitching him forward, hopelessly out of balance. The man gathered him in as he slid, twisted him round and forced his arm hard up between his shoulders. Colin gasped in agony and went down on his knees.

The man jerked him to his feet, turned him round again and slapped his face, viciously, with his free hand, again and again, until the boy's head was ringing with pain, his cheek a mass of flaming agony. He tried to duck, to kick out at his assailant, but the man knew all the tricks — and their counters. Savagely, the open-handed blows, with the force of trained muscles behind them, hammered into him, relentlessly.

He was barely conscious when a flurry of movement erupted somewhere near him and a woman's voice cried out shrilly.

'Stop it, Bert! Stop it! Let go of him!'

The rain of blows ceased, Colin's arm was freed. It fell numbly at his side. He tottered, almost fell. The man grabbed him again, but this time only to steady him.

'Bloody young nit!' he growled. 'Sneaking around here!'

'No need to knock him about like that, though,' the woman said sharply. 'Flew off the handle again, didn't you? If you'd only learn a bit of self-control — '

'Aw, can it, Gaye! What d'you expect me to do when I find him on the snoop? Kiss him and ask him in for supper?'

'You can bring him inside, at any rate,' a third voice said coldly from the lighted doorway. 'I want to talk to him. Come on, get moving!'

Colin blinked his vision clear from the tears of pain which had clouded it. His cheek felt as if it had been set on fire but the buzzing in his head began to quieten. He was able to think.

He'd got himself into a proper mess, no doubt about that. And he'd have to talk himself out of it, somehow. He told himself sternly to keep calm and use his loaf, advice which was easy enough to give . . .

'Move!' his captor ordered. He gave

Colin a shove towards the back door. Colin went forward. The man in the doorway stepped aside, gestured with his thumb at a room which gave on to the passage. As Colin obeyed the signal he heard the dustbin lid being replaced. The man who had given the orders followed him into the room, with the big fellow at his heels.

It was a brightly-furnished, comfortable apartment with a settee and easy chairs, a television set and a bowl of flowers on a central table. Colin guessed it was the staff sitting room. Another gesture ordered him to use the settee. The short stout man with the silver hair who made that gesture stepped to the empty fireplace and stood with his back to it. Colin recognised him now as Martin Pelford, the Healthways proprietor. He had seen him the previous day, talking to Inspector Dykes and Sergeant Garrett. An escape line of argument began to build up in Colin's mind.

Pelford said, 'Well, young man, I think you'd better start explaining yourself.' He spoke mildly enough, and his spectacles glinted as he turned his head sideways. 'By the way, haven't I seen you before recently?'

'You have, sir.' Colin was pleased that his words came out steadily. 'I came here yesterday with the two policemen. I waited outside in the car.'

'Ah! Of course. But it's unusual, surely, for police officers to take a young fellow like you around with them?'

'Well, you see, I reported — ' He was suddenly overtaken by a prolonged fit of coughing. He'd just been about to spill all the beans, which could have got Bailey, the gardener, into trouble, to say nothing of Keith Jackson and himself. The strict truth was definitely not the line to take here.

'Sorry,' he apologised and took out a rather grubby handkerchief to wipe his eyes. He flinched as his fingers touched his swollen cheek. 'I'm staying at the caravan site on Northway Road,' he went on, 'and I was having a walk up this way yesterday morning, and I passed your gates and thought I saw that gunman the police are looking for, walking about your grounds. The police had shown us an identikit picture, you see. So I reported to them and they came to investigate and brought me with them in case I'd be needed to identify the man I thought I'd seen.'

'But all this doesn't explain why we have caught you trespassing here tonight, does it?'

'And,' the big man put in, 'he was standing on that bin, looking in here, Mr. Pelford. And slipped off the lid, which was why we heard him.'

Colin turned to look at him.

'You've got your facts wrong,' he said. He still hated this man who had knocked him about so cruelly. 'Seems to me you're one of these pin-heads who acts first and thinks second.'

'I'm not taking that line of talk — ' He came thrusting forward but Pelford waved him back, frowning at Colin.

'Impertinence won't help you, young man. By the way, what is your name?'

'Colin Taylor.' He couldn't see any reason for refusing to give it, especially as he had the rest of his story worked out now.

'Well, Colin, carry on, please.'

'The police were convinced I'd made a mistake, sir, after they'd been here and talked to you.' He grinned lopsidedly. 'Made me feel a bit of a fool, actually. Anyway, I happened to be walking along the road outside just now, when a car pulled up ahead of me and a man got out and went through your gates. It struck me as a bit funny he didn't drive up to the house. When I came level with the gates I saw he was standing just inside, sort of studying the house. Then he crossed the lawn towards the back door and — well, I followed him.'

'With what idea in mind, exactly?'

'I thought he was acting queer, as if he didn't want to be seen — that sort of thing. It's difficult to put into words. So I got a bit curious, you see.'

'He wasn't a plainclothes policeman?' Pelford put the question sharply.

'Definitely no, sir.'

'And why are you so sure of that?'

'Well, because . . . ' Colin hesitated,

annoyed with himself for his thoughtless assertion. He didn't want, for some reason which wasn't at all clear in his own mind, to tell this man who Read was and where he had come from. 'Because he didn't strike me as one. I mean, he was acting' — he paused again to search for a word, found it and brought it out triumphantly — 'furtively.'

Above his glasses, Pelford's brows drew together.

'So you followed him. And what did he do?'

'He came round to the back here. When I got as far as that archway, he was standing on the dustbin, trying to look through the window. Then somebody seemed to approach the window, he stepped back quickly and fell off the bin. And you know the rest.'

'You had sneaked into the yard meanwhile. Why?'

'So he wouldn't see me if he turned round. The light from the window was shining on to the archway.'

The big man spoke. 'I didn't see any fellow when I went out. Only you, sonny.'

'Because by then he'd dodged away through the archway. You only saw me, and without giving me a chance to explain myself you attacked me.' The memory of it caused a resurgence of anger in Colin. 'Unprovoked assault, that was. And it's not legal.'

'Really!' Pelford spread his hands. 'My dear young friend, you've no cause to be talking about breaking laws! Mr. Canning here was only doing what any man would do with trespassers and Peeping Toms around.'

'He went for me, an' all,' Canning muttered. 'I had to do something, didn't I, in self-defence?'

'Quite correct,' Pelford agreed. 'And now, Master Taylor, we'll be glad to see the back of you. And take my advice, forget any aspirations you have of becoming a private sleuth. Especially round my property. Mr. Canning will escort you as far as the front gates.'

Colin was glad enough to go. A persistent ache was holding court inside his skull, he didn't like these people a bit, he was fed-up now with the idea of finding out more about Read and his friends. He got up and walked to the door without a word.

In silence, too, he went round the house and down the drive, with Canning a half-step behind him. He wouldn't have been surprised if the big ape had had another go at him, now they were away from Pelford's restraint and in the darkness together. But they reached the gates without incident — and just at the moment when a woman pushed them open from the road side.

She stopped and looked at them.

'Oh! I was just coming to have a word with Mr. Pelford.'

Canning peered at her, frowning.

'You shouldn't have come — ' He bit off the sentence. 'I mean, it's pretty late, isn't it, to be calling?'

'I couldn't get here any earlier, as you very well know.'

Canning turned to Colin. 'On your way now — sharp!'

Colin obeyed. He walked rapidly off, wondering where he had seen the woman before. He was almost home when he remembered. She was the box-office attendant at the Palladium. He'd seen the show twice and couldn't be mistaken. Besides, her photograph had been in the local paper after the Palladium hold-up.

It was nearly eleven when he reached the caravan, but his parents were not back. Colin shrugged, bathed his head and face in cold water and went to bed.

13

The Blue Lion, on the foreshore, standing back between a bingo hall and a fish and chip restaurant, had been patronised by generations of Whitsea fishermen. During the season it was inevitable that a large proportion of its customers were holiday-makers, and in order to keep a flow of their money directed to his till, the landlord had added some touches of local colour. A ship's lantern hung from the ceiling, fishing nets decorated the walls of the bar, several lobster pots were displayed on stands, and a ship's chronometer, above the bar, was ostentatiously referred to by the landlord when he inflated his lungs to shout, 'Last orders, gentlemen, please!'

The trippers, as the seafaring men called them, did not put the regular patrons off. Indeed, they were welcomed, for many more free drinks found their way down the throats of Whitsea natives in the season than out of it. When, in September, the coloured promenade lights were taken down, the donkeys returned to their winter pastures and the seaside landladies reckoned up their spoils, the Blue Lion's lantern was taken down, the nets and lobster pots stowed away. Only the chronometer ticked on when the gale-driven winter waves lashed at the pier and Whitsea lay sunk in out-of-season somnolence.

But this was August, and when Garrett stepped into the Blue Lion's bar that Monday evening, trade was brisk and voices were loud. A brief wait at the counter gained him a pint of bitter, and he was lucky enough to find a seat near the door.

He looked carefully around for the man Sergeant Prior had described to him — Puffer Tenby, the snout Prior was keen to have watched. Puffer had come up with the whisper of a bank raid in prospect, but Prior, with that sixth sense a successful C.I.D. man must acquire, was disinclined to believe the information. Though precautions had been taken,

Prior had a notion that the said whisper was a cover-up for another operation and he was anxious to get on the track of it. Garrett had promised to do what he could to help, and the Blue Lion, Puffer's usual port of call, was the obvious starting point.

No little man in a blue jersey, with a trick of puffing out his lips at the end of his sentences, was in evidence, however.

The three men who shared Garrett's table were chattering away in Tyneside accents he found almost incomprehensible. They took no notice of him. He sat and sipped, sipped and watched. His glass was empty and he was reluctantly deciding he had better have a refill when the door opened and a man came in.

Garrett at once dropped the rolled-up newspaper he had been idly tapping against his knee, and bent floorwards to grope for it. He didn't want the newcomer to see him, for this was Kendall from the caravan site. He wore a high-necked black sweater which concealed the plaster on his neck. He stood just inside the room, his keen, handsome face alert as he looked around the place. The alertness was replaced by a frown, and Garrett guessed Kendall had expected to meet someone there, someone who hadn't turned up yet.

The door opened again, shoved by a small figure which Garrett knew must be that of Puffer Tenby. Puffer headed for the counter, moving quickly, then, as he was passing Kendall, he stumbled and would have fallen if the other had not shot out a hand to steady him. Kendall began to apologise profusely, glancing down at his out-thrust foot. Puffer looked aggrieved, scowled up at him, his lips working in and out. There was only one possible conclusion to the situation. Kendall gestured towards the bar and Puffer nodded and followed him up to the counter.

Pints were drawn and served to them and they seemed to fall into casual chat as they stood there drinking. Garrett would have liked to tune into that conversation, but Kendall had seen him before, it was possible he knew Garrett for a policeman. And this was a fact which must not be mentioned to his companion, Puffer Tenby.

But the friendly get-together did not last long. Puffer nodded at something Kendall said, then drained his glass in two long swallows. He put it down, turned and made for the door. Garrett let him get outside before he, too, sought the fresh air.

Puffer had turned to his right and was now hurrying past the bingo hall, past a shop which sold toys and fancy goods. Beyond this was an amusement arcade, into which Puffer dived. Garrett set out to follow him.

The place was moderately full of people of all ages playing the wide range of machines. Garrett edged his way in and began to move around, looking for Puffer.

He found the little man at a pin-table, one of a row of six, all in use. Puffer was standing behind the two youths who were playing, watching them impatiently as if he were eager to have a go himself. When they moved away he jumped forward, thrust a coin into the slot. But when the balls came up he seemed to lose his interest. He sent one steel sphere shooting up the board but Garrett saw he wasn't watching its progress. Instead, his small eyes were darting from side to side, away from the game.

Garrett saw Molly Bilton, luckily, before she could spot him. She came through the entrance, stood there a moment as if she were giving the place a general look-over, then walked straight across to the pin-table where Puffer was. She took up a position behind him, he looked round, said something to her and at once began to play quickly. The balls scuttled up the board, lights flashed on and off, the score flicked in its indicator. Molly spoke to Puffer, he nodded, went on playing. To all appearances, here was a young woman wanting to try her luck, and an undersized middle-aged man reassuring her he wouldn't keep her waiting more than a few seconds.

Puffer shot his last ball, glanced at the score, turned away with a shrug. Molly took his place. He stood by her, chatting for a moment or two, then he walked out into the street. Garrett, who had concealed himself behind a pillar, slipped out after him. Puffer turned to his left, Garrett walked casually across the road to the railing-edged sidewalk opposite. He watched Puffer re-enter the Blue Lion. He had hardly disappeared within when Molly came out of the arcade. She turned in the opposite direction.

It was easy for Garrett to keep observation on her from his side of the road. The strolling groups of people gave him cover without obstructing his view. It was Puffer whom he had promised to keep tabs on, but Puffer, he judged, was likely to stay put now for a while, and Garrett was more interested in Molly Bilton.

She walked some fifty yards before she halted by a parked car. Its driver leaned across to open the passenger's door, Molly got in with a flash of immaculately-nyloned legs. The door was closed, the engine started and the car pulled out into the traffic stream. Garrett saw it was Kendall's car, he caught a glimpse of the man at the wheel. The couple drove off in the direction of Molly's hotel.

Garrett returned to the Blue Lion. Puffer was still there, one of a group of locals who had established themselves in a corner round a circular table. Garrett bought a drink and wandered across the crowded bar room towards the table. He leaned against the wall nearby, having Puffer's back to him. The group was discussing, with considerable heat, the iniquities of the 'Dutchies' who trawled over nets and took no notice of legal fishing limits. Garrett listened for several minutes to complaints of small catches by local fishermen and assertions that 'the Gov'ment did ought to do something about it.' Puffer Tenby's only contributions to the discussion were a series of wise-seeming nods. He sipped occasionally at his pint, and it was clear now that he intended to make that pint last out just as long as ever he could.

Garrett finished his own drink and left the pub. He turned towards a bus stop, confident he would gather no further information for Sergeant Prior that night. The bus set him down near the caravan site entrance, it was twenty minutes past ten, late enough, but Garrett wasn't inclined to go home before he had taken one quick walk through the site. After all, he'd promised to keep an eye on it.

He considered himself fortunate not to run into Grinstead, the warden, at that time of night. Though he'd had no definite instructions on the point, he judged Inspector Dykes would prefer Grinstead to be unaware his charge was still under police observation. Most of the vans were in darkness, Kendall's car was back in place but Read's was absent. Garrett went on to the far end of the area, to the Taylors' caravan. That, too, showed no light.

He made his way towards Cliffside, supper and bed. Tomorrow, Prior would be interested in his report. Garrett was not to know that the morrow would prove so busy for Prior that he wouldn't care a tinker's cuss for the doings of Puffer Tenby on the previous evening.

14

Robert Sheldon was in his mid-forties, a chunky man, not tall, with a barrel-like chest and thick arms and legs. His black hair was thinning on top but this was concealed by the cap he always wore, a little to one side of his head. He was slow-moving, slow of speech, but there was intelligence and a touch of humour in his brown eyes. He worked for John Palmer, of Barwell Farm, a ninety acre property some two miles inland from Whitsea. At eight-fifteen that Tuesday morning he pushed open the gate of a field known as Crow Hill where his morning's work literally lay before him.

They'd had Crow Hill in oats that year, and the field was too small, too awkwardly shaped, to put in a combine. So they'd had to get the old binder out of the barn and rattle round with that. The cutting had been finished late the previous evening, and the boss had said the tied sheaves could lie where they were for the night. Bob Sheldon could shuck them up when he'd done milking in the morning.

Crow Hill was an old pasture, ploughed up two years previously. Near the gate, and backing on the road was an open-fronted wooden shed of tarred boards and a roof of corrugated iron, originally a cattle shelter. Bob hadn't liked the look of the sky that morning, rain was about, he was sure. He'd brought his old mac along with his mid-morning 'snap.' He closed the gate and went across to the shed to dump his impedimenta in the dry.

The man's body was lying face downwards in an untidy heap just inside the shed, on the old, discoloured straw which carpeted it. Bob swore with surprise and shock, dropped his mac and snap-bag, and went reluctantly forward. He bent and grasped the sweatered sleeve of one outflung arm. He lifted, and the arm came up like a dried stick. Bob straightened himself, wiped his fingers on his corduroy trousers. He picked up his tackle and went back to the gate, pulling it wide open and hanging his stuff, out of the way, on the gatepost. He couldn't imagine himself wanting a mid-morning snack that day, anyway.

He stepped forward to the edge of the road, busy with the morning traffic. He'd got to stop one of those cars, but they were all helling along at speed and no driver would be likely to take notice of a chap on the roadside making signals. He gave a small grunt of relief when he saw the Royal Mail van appear in the distance. That would be Jim Robertson on his way back to head office from his morning round. Bob waited until the red van neared him, then stepped out and waved it down.

Jim Robertson wasted no time either with senseless questions or useless comment.

'I'll ring from the box opposite the entrance to Green Lane,' he said and was moving again inside thirty seconds.

Bob watched him go, then turned back to the field. There was going to be a heck of a lot of tramping about this part of it before long — vehicles coming in as well. Better start moving a few sheaves out of the way before they got beat into nothing and all that corn lost. Then he remembered one shouldn't touch anything in a case like this. There might be tracks or something. He stood where he was, waiting patiently.

Before five minutes had gone he saw the prowl car coming. Its driver pulled up opposite Bob, he and his mate got out of the car. Bob said his piece, waving a hand towards the shed. The patrolmen nodded, told him to stick around. Bob walked up the hedge a distance, well out of the way, picked up a sheaf in each hand, slammed the butts into the ground at the correct angle, and with the knots of the binder twine around them facing outwards. A quick shake intermingled their heads. He bent for another two. Dead men or not, that field had to be put up, and the more he did before the rain came, the better.

Inspector Dykes received the call as he was regarding, with some distaste, the morning contents of his 'In' tray. He pushed this aside and buzzed for Sergeant

Prior. He, too, was not averse to a trip outside the office. The police surgeon, the camera and fingerprints men were alerted. Dykes drove the radio-controlled car expertly through the town traffic and put his foot down when they cleared the speed-restricted area. They were on the scene so quickly that the patrolmen had to do a hasty nip of the cigarettes they had lit, as one of them remarked, 'to take the taste of that in yonder out of our mouths.'

Dykes heard their report and he and Prior took over. One look at the corpse inside the shed sent Dykes back to his car, to call up more assistance. He found the ambulance had arrived, and ordered it to stand by. One of the patrol crew was instructed to fetch Bob Sheldon across.

Dykes listened to his story, glad to find this seemed to be a fellow with a bit of commonsense. He didn't waste words.

'You took a look at this man,' Dykes said. 'Obviously, you don't know who he is, or you'd have said so.'

'That's right, sir. Perfect stranger to me.'

'When were you last in the shed there?'

'Half past nine last night, sir.'

'H'm — that was rather late, wasn't it?'

'We cut this field yesterday with the tractor and binder. That's to say, I cut it. Mr. Palmer, my boss, was here with me. It was quite a bit after eight when we finished. Mr. Palmer said we'd call it a day, I took the tackle back and went home for my supper. Then I remembered I'd left an old haversack full of tools in yon shed — we'd been having a bit of trouble with the tractor yesterday. So I came along to pick 'em up. I live at yon cottage down the road.'

'Good!' Dykes said. 'That helps us to fix times. The shed was quite normal then?'

Sheldon nodded.

'This road,' Dykes went on, 'won't be particularly busy during the night, I suppose?'

'No sir. Traffic slacks off about ten, this time of year. Later than that, it's likely that a chap in a car, wanting to dump a body, could drive in through the gate and up to the shed, and away again without being seen.'

'You think that's what happened, Mr. Sheldon?'

'I expect you'll have noticed the tyre tracks from that gate to the shed. They're a bit faint in the stubble, but you can see 'em, and where a car has run over some of the sheaves. My boss drove his Land Rover up here yesterday but he didn't take it anywhere near the shed — besides, those aren't either Rover nor yet tractor marks. And when I got here this morning the gate wasn't properly fastened, like I left it. And the way that poor chap's lying — well, it looks as if somebody just chucked him down there.' He glanced at the sky. 'Starting to rain, sir. I'd like to get on, if you don't mind.'

'All right, and thanks.' Dykes turned back to the gate. A dark green M.G. convertible roared up, its driver braking sharply behind the waiting ambulance. He sprang out, a tall, lean young man whose movements suggested he was late for some important appointment already and hadn't a moment to spare.

'Hi, Dykes! Where's the cold meat?'

Dykes said, 'Morning, doctor. If you'll come this way . . .'

The police surgeon, Dr. Burroughs, spoke to the two ambulance men. 'Shove the hood up over that heap of mine, will you, lads? I haven't had a wet seat since I was a kid, and fibrositis in the gluteus maximus — backside to you — can be painful.' He followed Dykes to the shed, skirting the tarpaulins Prior had slready put down to cover the wheel marks. The rain was falling steadily now.

Inside the shed, Baber, the camera technician, was unscrewing a used flash bulb while Collins, the 'dabs' expert, stood idly aside.

'Can't chalk round the bodd here,' he said to Dykes. 'I suppose we could do an outline with pegs — if we had any pegs.'

'Doesn't matter,' Dykes replied. 'You found anything, Cox?'

The detective constable who was moving carefully about the shed shook his head. 'No evidence, sir, least, not in plain sight. I suppose all this floor litter could be shifted — big job, though.'

'It may not be necessary. Well, doctor?'

Burroughs stood up, dusting off the knees of his olive-green slacks.

'Manual strangulation,' he said. 'Neck's broken, too. No rigor in the legs yet — he seems quite healthy, and that, plus the fact he was choked to death, is likely to hold rigor up.' He shook his head. 'Not earlier than midnight is all I can venture to say at this point. Can we get him aboard and away?'

Dykes nodded. The ambulance men came and went away, loaded. The squad car was sent back to its normal duties, Baber packed up his photographic equipment. Dykes looked at his small team.

'Nothing more for us here, I think. We'll need a man on guard — sergeant?'

'I've already called in, sir. A constable's coming out on a motor-bike.'

'Good. We'll get back to H.Q., start ringing around the divisions in case they've had any 'missing' reports. You took his prints, of course, Collins?'

He received a sour nod. Collins prided himself on doing his job without the need of supplementary orders.

'Sooner you take 'em after death,

clearer they always are,' he grunted. 'I'll check with C.R.O., of course. That's routine,' he added, just in case Inspector Dykes didn't know.

'There's a bit of a break in the sky towards the west,' Detective Constable Cox said. He was standing in the shed entrance, looking out. 'Rain'll be over soon. Not before that chap gets proper wet, though.'

He jerked a thumb outwards. Dykes stepped to his side and saw Bob Sheldon trying to find shelter against a cut-down, gappy hedge. Dykes called him over and Bob came at once.

'We're finished here, Mr. Sheldon. No need for you to stay out in the rain.'

'Shan't be sorry to get under cover, sir. I brought a mac, but left it on the gate there. Thought I'd better not come and get it — you'd want me out of the way.'

'Yes. Well, we're leaving those tarps in place, and a man will be along to stand guard. We'll need a statement from you, for the record. I'll send somebody along later. I suppose you haven't thought of anything else that might be useful to us?'

'Just one thing, sir. As I was going back home last night, after fetching my tool bag, a motor-bike with a young couple on it came cruising along, like, towards this field. When I turned into my own gate at home I looked back, and they were stopped opposite here and he was saying something to her, and the thought did pass through my mind they were looking for somewhere to shack up for a while and had spotted the shed. Young couples often do use it, and nobody minds. We were all young once, and courting couples don't do any harm to a place like this. Their minds are on other things, like.' He shook his head. 'You're going to ask me if I can describe 'em, or the bike. They were too far away. Sorry.'

'If they used this place, they could have been the ones who left the gate not properly fastened.'

'Could have been, but I doubt it, sir. It isn't the easiest of gates to open, and a pair like that, they'd likely be in a fairish hurry. They'd leave the bike parked on the grass verge and climb over the gate.'

Dykes nodded absently, his eyes on the

motor-cycle which had drawn up on the road. A uniformed constable dismounted and received his orders. As Dykes and Prior headed the small official motorcade back to Whitsea the rain stopped and the sun came out.

'It's obvious you're dying to say something, sergeant,' Dykes said when, having gone into top, he took his hand from the gear lever. 'Better get it off your chest. I wish there was somebody here to bet me I don't know what it is, too.'

Prior gave a sideways grin.

'I guessed you'd spot it, sir. Or course, when a man's been strangled it does make a difference to his features. Yet I thought it was unmistakable. Tall man, too, and about the estimated age. I frisked him while you were talking to the farm hand, but he wasn't carrying his gun.'

'So we get the Kendalls to see if they can identify him as the man who shot at Kendall. Correction. We'll ask Kendall himself to do that job. I wouldn't like to force a woman to look at that body. And supposing we do get a firm assurance he is the gunman of the caravan site, how much further on are we?'

'He won't do any more shooting up on our patch, anyway.'

'Cold comfort, Prior. However, we'll have to go all out on it.' They exchanged no further words until the car slid into its parking slot at Whitsea Central.

Prior and Cox followed Dykes to the inspector's office. Cox was carrying a plastic bag which he put on the table.

'Contents of his pockets, sir.'

'Tip 'em out.'

There was a crumpled handkerchief, a folding leather notecase which held six pound notes, the stub of a ticket for the back stalls of Whitsea's Regal Cinema. A pocket knife with its small blade broken, some loose change, half a roll of mint sweets and a biro pen completed the tally.

'No wallet,' Cox pointed out, 'so no personal identification.'

Dykes waved at the small pile. 'Put them back and stow them away. Then drive over to the caravan site and see if you can get hold of Kendall. Take him to the morgue and treat him to a look at the body. If Mrs. Kendall is on the site, you can drop a hint that a double identification would be valuable, but don't press it if she isn't keen.'

As the door closed behind Cox, Dykes turned to Prior.

'There's just a possibility a patrolman passed along that road last night and saw the parked motor-bike Sheldon mentioned. See if you can find out about this. Then you'd better take some stuff out to the shed again and cast those tyre tracks. Okay?'

Prior nodded and left. Dykes glanced at his watch and saw it was time for a mid-morning drink. He rang the main office, and when a police cadet came, he asked, 'Is Mr. Spratt on the premises, do you know?'

'He is, sir, I was just going to ask him if I could take him a coffee.'

'Never ask inspectors a question like that, Mason. Just take 'em one. In this case you can bring two from the canteen and then tell Mr. Spratt I'd be glad if he could join me here.'

Spratt was only too ready to accept the

invitation. He'd spent another half-morning of getting nowhere. Nothing new had broken to help him, he had gone over the details of the Burleigh Hotel robbery again without finding a single lead. For the past thirty minutes he had been debating with himself if his best move would be to ring Hallam in Deniston and ask for a recall. That meant owning himself beaten, but Spratt had always put common-sense before self-pride. He had been in Whitsea almost three days without a single result to show. It didn't suit him to sit in a comfortable chair in Whitsea, doing little or nothing. But he put his problems aside as he joined Dykes and picked up a coffee cup.

'Why the honour, Charles?' he asked his host.

'I thought you might like to hear about the job which turned up this morning.' Briefly, Dykes gave the facts. 'It isn't your pigeon, I know, Jack,' he finished, 'but I thought you might be interested. I'm just waiting for — ' His telephone rang.

'Collins here,' a gruff voice said. 'C.R.O. has done a quick check for me. The bloke's name is Raymond Lever, alias Ronald Lawson, alias James Carr. Normal territory the Midlands. Birmingham, Leicester, Nottingham. Four stretches, all for safe-breaking. Physical and career details to follow.'

'That's great!' Dykes said enthusiastically. 'You must have done a good printing job on him, Terry. Believe me, I'm very — '

He put the handset back on its studs and grinned at Spratt.

'He cut me off. There's rank-respect for you! But Collins is one of the best in the business, and I'm lucky to have him. We've identified our man, Jack.' He passed across the notes he had been making as Collins reported.

'Another form-merchant to add to friend Pelford,' Spratt said. 'This could help me, too. Although,' he added, 'there's that point about none of the robberies involving a safe-breaking.'

'Lever told the Kendalls he'd come from Leeds. Maybe his idea was to join this gang. We didn't find a wallet on him, so no personal papers. He wasn't robbed of his money. His killer could have taken the wallet, though. There's a numbered ticket stub from one of the local cinemas among his stuff. It's possible we can find out when he saw the show. He arrived here on Saturday, so there are only three days to cover. He could have met somebody at the cinema, not that it's fair to expect an usherette to remember . . . I'm just talking it out to myself, Jack.'

'It's not a bad way,' Spratt replied, as Mason, the cadet, followed his knock into the room. 'P.C. Walters is here, sir,' he said. 'He was on motor-cycle patrol along Faynor Road last night.'

'Send him in, please.' Dykes added to Spratt, 'You needn't go unless you want to, Jack.'

'Ratepayers' money,' Spratt returned. 'I'd better try to earn some of it.' In the doorway he met a young, fair-haired man in civilian clothes, whose hand started to jerk up in a salute until its owner remembered he wasn't dressed for it. He stood aside with a friendly, 'Good morning, sir!' then went into Dykes' room.

'You wanted to see me, sir?'

Dykes waved him to a chair.

'You came off duty at six this morning, Walters?'

'Yes sir. I'm on nights this week.'

'Then you'll be cursing me for dragging you in here when you're due for some sleep.'

'That's okay, sir. I never get down to it before midday. I understand it's about the Faynor Road patrol I did last night?'

Dykes nodded, and told him why. Before he had finished he saw by the expression on Walters' face that the constable had something to tell him.

'Just turned eleven, sir, I was on my way out to Faynor village which is my patrol limit. I noticed a motor-cycle parked in a field gateway, and there is a shed just inside the field. I thought I'd better check. I stopped, went into the field and up to the shed. I heard movement inside and shone my lamp. I found a young couple there, teenagers. I told them it was time they were on their way home. The fellow said okay, they were just going. I went on to Faynor, I've a point to make there with one of the Faynor constables.

'I was talking to this chap — his name's Holt — when the youth I'd spoken to at the shed came along on his bike. Holt pulled him up, he had a message for this lad's father. The lad said to me, joking, like, that I'd have a chance to disturb another courting couple in the shed. He'd taken his girl into Whitsea, where she lives, and on the way back he'd seen a car pulled up by the field gate. But it wasn't there when I went by on my way back, which would be about ten to twelve, sir.'

Dykes looked up from the note-pad he was using.

'How did you get into the field?'

'Over the gate, sir. It was fastened up a bit awkwardly, it was quicker to climb it, both going and coming back.'

'And that's the lot?'

'Yes, sir. Doesn't help much, I suppose?'

'It could help quite a lot, Walters. You haven't wasted your off-duty time coming here. And thanks.'

When Walters had gone he picked up

his telephone and put a call through to the superintendent in charge of the county division which included the village of Faynor. Receiving permission to go ahead, by all means, he had Police Constable Holt's number rung. Holt had retired to bed, but sounded quite cheerful when Dykes put his request.

'The lad's name is Stephen Ockley, sir,' he replied. 'Works in the local garage here. Steady, reliable chap, a bit too fond of the girls, maybe, but that's just his age. You'd like to see him personally? Right, sir. My wife'll go down to the garage straight away with the message.'

Cox rang in to report that Kendall, at the mortuary, had been 'almost sure' the dead man, was the one they had brought from Pickering to Whitsea and who later invaded his caravan. The doctor's preliminary report came in — Burroughs was a quick worker. Manual strangulation confirmed — neck could have been broken when the body was thrown down in the shed. Stomach contents suggested death an hour after a light supper — details of identifiable food taken herewith. Clothing, finger-nail scrapings, etc., passed to County Forensic.

Dykes put the report on one side and considered Kendall's 'almost sure' identification. Was it good enough, taken in connection with the C.R.O. findings? Or should he ask that girl from Healthways, Miss Henson, to check if it was the man she had seen on Sunday morning? The gardener, Bailey, had also seen him. Dykes went along the corridor to Superintendent Welling's room.

Welling considered the point. 'Depends on whether the coroner will accept it, and you know old Morley. Proper devil for identification. I'll have a word with him, though. You mark time on it for the moment.'

Relieved of this problem, Dykes sought his own office again. A duty constable was just putting a flimsy on his desk.

'Hot off the teleprinter, sir. Details of the man Lever.'

'Thanks.' Dykes sat down to study them. He skipped the physical items but gave some study to the potted history of Lever which C.R.O. had supplied. The man had been a first-class safe-breaker, no doubt about that. And, Dykes reflected, one could guess he had not come to Whitsea merely for a holiday. The report said he had also, in the past, worked with Jack Bilton.

Inspector Spratt was going to be interested in that piece of information.

15

Garrett's first task that morning was to let Sergeant Prior know about Puffer Tenby's doings the previous evening. After breakfast he picked up the Cliffside telephone and dialled Whitsea Central. He was told Sergeant Prior, and Inspector Dykes, were out of town on a case. Garrett said he'd come in and make out a written report.

As he stepped out of the house Colin Taylor started towards him from the pavement opposite the gate where he had been waiting.

Garrett wasn't particularly pleased to see him. This lad had a half-excited, half-sheepish look which suggested he'd been poking his nose again into matters which were not his concern. And he was going to unload whatever it was on Sergeant Dick Garrett.

His premonition proved correct. To his forced smile and 'Well, look who's here!'

Colin returned a hesitant grin.

'Excuse me, Mr. Garrett, but I'd like to talk to you. I've been waiting here hoping to see you.'

'You should have come to the house,' Garrett returned. 'Anyway, I'm walking into town, so if you've nothing better to do you can come along and we'll talk as we go. What's it all about this time?'

Colin fell into step beside him. 'I think I have some information the police ought to know about.'

'Then why not take it directly to them?'

'Well, it's a bit awkward, you see.'

Garrett gave a brief, unamused grin. 'Which means you've been acting the famous private eye again, I suppose? And got yourself into more trouble?'

Colin reddened. 'Sorry. Forget it, Mr. Garrett. Just let's pretend I never mentioned the subject.' The asperity in his voice matched that in Garrett's own. 'I'll leave you here and go down to the beach.'

Impulsively, Garrett put a hand on his shoulder.

'Sorry, lad. I didn't mean you to take it

that way. Just you tell me all about it, man to man, like.'

Colin was his former self at once. 'It's like this. I was coming back last night to the caravan . . . '

He went on to tell Garrett what he had heard outside the Kendalls' van, and how — just for a giggle, he interpolated — he'd legged it out to Healthways, had followed Read into the grounds. How Read had been spying there and how he himself had been caught. And, when the man Canning had been seeing him off the premises, how they had practically run into the woman from the Palladium box-office.

Long before he had finished Garrett had steered him into one of the smaller, well-kept public gardens for which Whitsea is noted. They found a seat in a secluded corner and when Colin ended his story Garrett turned sideways to face him.

'Right. Now let's work it all out backward, as it were. Does everything seem normal at those two vans this morning?' Colin nodded. 'I walked past them on my way out. Didn't see anything unusual. Both the families seemed to be having breakfast — that was all.'

'This woman you saw visiting Healthways. You're sure she was the one from the Palladium? And when I say sure, I mean dead sure, without a shadow of doubt?'

'Certain of it. I got a good look at her in the lamplight. I've bought tickets from her twice, and I saw her picture in the paper. I couldn't be mistaken.'

'And Read was on the spy at Healthways. He got away, and you were caught. Did you see him, or his car, again that night?'

'No, Mr. Garrett. It wasn't where he'd parked it before he went into Healthways — I did notice that. I didn't see it at the site when I got back — I mean, I forgot to notice if it was there or not. I was pretty tired, my head was just about splitting and I was in a hurry to get to bed before my parents came back and asked me what had happened to my face. It was still a bit red and swollen, you see.'

While Colin had talked, Garrett had

been scribbling shorthand notes on the back of a used envelope. He glanced down at them.

'This chap Canning sounds quite a tearaway. There wasn't any reason to go for you as he did. Look, did Mr. Pelford seem at all worried when you told him Read had been spying?'

'I couldn't tell. I didn't mention Read's name to him. I think he accepted my story as to why I was there, though.'

'You probably did quite a good job when you made him think the police had decided your report of seeing that gunman at Healthways wasn't true.'

'I still think I did see him, Mr. Garrett.'

'We'll leave that for the moment. Now, let's go back over the conversation you heard outside the Kendalls' caravan. That could be important if — and don't take this the wrong way — if it's accurate.'

'I've told you just what I heard. I haven't made anything up.'

Garrett grinned. 'I'll check that, in a policemanlike manner. Just let's have it all again from you.'

'The first person I heard speaking was

Mrs. Read . . . ' Garrett listened to the re-run of Colin's narrative, his eyes on his notes. ' . . . And when Mrs. Kendall said Mr. Read had time for another coffee, and he agreed, I left.'

'Good.' Garrett jumped up. 'Now, you leave all this with me. I'm on my way to see one of the local C.I.D. men, and I'll hand this stuff over to whoever it may concern. See you again sometime.'

He walked away, deliberately ignoring the expectant look on Colin's face. He knew the lad had hoped for an invitation to accompany him to Headquarters, but that just wasn't on, in Garrett's view. Not yet, anyway. Besides, he wasn't in a hurry himself to get there. He strolled through the streets, read the papers in the municipal library. It was late in the morning when he reached Whitsea Central.

The duty sergeant shook his head when Garrett asked if Sergeant Prior had returned.

'He hasn't. Bloke got himself killed in a shed on the Faynor Road last night. Result — all the Brains Department are on panic stations.' He gave Garrett the details.

'Inspector Spratt, then? Is he in?' Garrett asked.

'Oh, he's around somewhere. In that room he's using, I expect. Know your way there?'

Garrett said he did. He found Spratt at his desk, and glad, apparently, to see his Deniston colleague. His expression of pleasure heightened when he heard what Garrett had to tell him.

'I wonder, without being too optimistic, if this is the lead I've been hoping for?' he said. 'Let's have that bit again where the lad heard Read talking about the pickings.'

''If he's there, we can bet he's blown on us and Pelford can walk in and take the pickings after all the trouble we've had setting the job up. But if he isn't at Healthways we can go ahead,'' Garrett read.

'Right. And young Taylor heard the name Molly mentioned?'

'Yes. He didn't seem to connect her with the woman who'd given her name as

236

Molly Brown. But Molly met Puffer Tenby last night, and had some conversation with him, after Kendall had told him where to find her. Which ties Molly up with those two families on the site, at any rate.'

'And with your friend Puffer. Yet he's supposed to be a snout — helping our side. I wonder if Mr. Dykes — '

It was a case of talking of the devil. Dykes walked into the room at that moment. He nodded pleasantly to Garrett.

'Couple of additional details on the dead man, Lever,' he told Spratt. 'Kendall, the caravan bloke, is practically certain he's the gunman we've been looking for. If he is, that's one job off my mind. The other thing, which should interest you, is that he once worked for Jack Bilton.'

'Did he now? That really does mean something. How busy are you at the moment?'

'Not very. I'm waiting to interview a young chap who's coming in from Faynor.'

'Then get an earful of this.' Spratt nodded to Garrett, who told his story once again.

'So,' Dykes said thoughtfully, 'we appear to have a definite tie-in here. Molly Bilton and the caravan lot. And, to repeat myself, the dead man was in Jack Bilton's organisation.' He turned towards Garrett. 'Sergeant Prior will be interested to hear of Puffer Tenby's doings last night. He's Prior's particular snout, and what Puffer's aim was, meeting Molly Bilton, is something Prior will have to puzzle over.'

'There's another point which strikes me, sir,' Garrett said. 'Colin Taylor saw the Kendalls arrive on Saturday, and you remember how definite he was they didn't put a man down outside the site. Now, I know this lad is inclined to push himself into spots he'd be better out of, but I do think he's an accurate observer. If he was right, and the Kendalls were pitching us a tale about meeting Lever at Pickering, it's possible Lever went into the site with them, and there was some sort of row leading to the shooting.'

Dykes considered this. 'In that case, would Kendall have identified him on the slab this morning? Why not say he'd never seen the chap before? Unless, of course, it was to his advantage in some way to identify him . . . Getting a trifle complicated, isn't it?'

'You had a good description of the gunman from Kendall's wife, didn't you?' Spratt put in. 'Maybe Kendall didn't want to raise suspicions by saying he had never seen the dead man before. If he's mixed up in some villany, either committed or about to be committed, he wouldn't say anything which might rouse the interest of the law.'

'What I'd like to do — ' Dykes paused, and Spratt called out, 'Come in,' to a knock at the door. A constable put his head in.

'Stephen Ockley, from Faynor, is here, Mr. Dykes.'

'Show him in, please. You won't mind, I'm sure,' he added to Spratt. 'I'd like you to hear what he has to say, if anything. You, too, sergeant.'

A youth in his late teens entered the

room. He was tall, whippily-built, with a snub nose, a wide mouth and a cheerful grin. He wore a leather jacket over an oil-stained boiler suit and a crash helmet swung from its chinstrap in one of his hands.

Dykes got up to place a chair. 'These officers are working with me, Mr. Ockley. It was good of you come in so promptly.'

The visitor's grin broadened. 'Any time off work goes with me, inspector. And I'd feel more comfortable if you faded out the 'Mr. Ockley' line. Steve's the tag, from one and all, if you don't mind.'

'Right, Steve. You know why I want to see you?'

'Haven't a clue, inspector. I was just told to get on the bike and come here ... Unless it's because I was in a shed with a bird last night? If that's a crime nowadays. But I'll swear on oath I never did anything that 'ud bring tears to me old mum's eyes. The bird wouldn't let me.'

Dykes spoke crisply.

'I believe you saw a car standing on the road opposite that shed on your way home last night?'

Ockley nodded. 'That's right. And I mentioned it to the Whitsea policeman who was talking to Bill Holt in our village when I rode in.'

'I'd like you to describe the car, Steve.'

Ockley's brows wrinkled in thought. 'That wouldn't be easy. I only caught a glimpse of it. There was a biggish car approaching, see, main beam full on. Some of 'em simply won't dip. I was cursing, I can tell you. I mean, on a road as well lit as that, and all. Anyway, I was checking it was safe to pull out and pass this parked car, so, as I say . . . No, sorry, I can't help. All I know is that it looked like a foreign job. Being in the trade, as I am, it's built-in, like, to notice cars, even if you aren't really looking, but I didn't see much of that one.'

'What about its colour?'

Ockley shook his head. 'You can't judge colours properly under those sodium lights.'

Dykes leaned forward to press a button on the desk. The cadet came in at once.

'Ask the duty sergeant for the vehicle

recognition book, please,' Dykes instructed. He turned to Ockley. 'You just saw the car — nobody in it or near it?'

'Just the car, inspector. 'Course, the fellow approaching would see it, too. But to me he was just a shape behind his blasted lights, so I couldn't help you to find him.'

'See what you can do with this.' The cadet had brought a large, thick book which Dykes laid, open, on the desk. Ockley got up and went to lean over it.

Each page carried pictures and drawings of cars, one make to each page. Besides representations of the complete vehicle from several angles, there were close-up details of features, such as radiator, grills, bumper-bars, wheels, bonnets, boots. There were also blacked-in drawings of shapes, fore, aft and sideways.

'The Young Constable's Bible — or one of 'em', Dykes explained. 'Take your time, Steve.'

Ockley seemed to know what he was looking for. He flicked most of the pages over with a mere glance, but others he studied more carefully. He reached the end of the book and began to turn the pages back again.

'This one,' he said. 'Mind, I'm not swearing to it in Court, but if that car wasn't a Saab, I'll eat my skid-lid.'

'Thanks,' Dykes said. 'It gives us a line to try, anyway.' He ushered Ockley to the door, thanked him again and closed the door behind him, leaning against it. He grinned at Garrett. 'I think I know what you're going to say!'

'Pelford owns a Saab, sir. We saw it on his drive on Sunday morning.'

'Quite. Which brings me back to what I was about to say when young Ockley arrived. I've got this murder job on hand. My men are all at full stretch. And I want somebody to talk to Pelford without delay. I want to know what Read was looking for there, but I'd rather not have him tackled directly yet. I want to know, also, why Beryl Graham was visiting Healthways last night.' He paused to look at Garrett hopefully. 'I can let you have the use of a car.'

'All right, sir. I'll do what I can. Of course . . . '

'Yes, sergeant?'

'I was just going to say that, as you know, two people are better than one on an inquiry of that sort. Still, if you can't spare anybody else . . . ' He kept his eyes steadfastly away from Spratt.

'Yes, it's a pity,' Dykes agreed, staring at the ceiling. 'And with all due respect, sergeant, a higher-ranking officer with you would strengthen your position enormously.'

'Just what I was thinking myself, sir.'

Spratt chuckled. 'You can come off it, both of you.' He gathered his papers together, slid them into a drawer and locked it. 'A trip out will do me the world of good. And we'll use my car.'

He and Garrett were on their way within five minutes.

'I was thinking it was time I had a glance at Pelford's set-up,' Spratt said. 'I suppose I'd better do most of the talking, too.'

'I'm hoping to get a close look at his car, sir. The tyre treads may still be holding some soil from that field, if it was the one which was driven in there. I might get a chance to take some specimens.'

So it was arranged that only Spratt should make the official call. The drive gates at Healthways were open and as the car moved up towards the house Garrett pointed to an arched entrance on their left.

'Access to the former stable yard, I'd say. That's where the garage is now. I'll have a stroll around there, and hope for the best.'

Spratt nodded, halting the car at the front steps. He got out, mounted the steps and rang the bell. The young woman whom Garrett had seen on his previous visit answered the door. Spratt was ushered inside.

Garrett waited for a few minutes before he opened the car door, swung his feet on to the gravel and stood upright. He paced back and forth several times, giving the impression, to anyone watching from the windows, of a man who was rapidly getting bored by having to hang about. He crossed to a rose bed and examined the bushes there. Then he began to wander casually towards the archway on the left.

On the concrete of the old stable yard the red Saab was standing. A big man in a tee-shirt, grey flannels and gum boots was washing the car. He was a tall man, well-built, muscular. He moved with the smooth balanced action of an athlete in training.

'Giving her a real good do, eh?' Garrett spoke loudly, to attract the man's attention. He let a wide, friendly grin accompany the words.

The other looked up swiftly and scowled at him.

'Who are you? What d'you want?'

Garrett shrugged. 'My boss is calling on Mr. Pelford. I'm just hanging around waiting for him. Nice car you have here.'

'And who is your boss, and what's he come for?'

Garrett ignored the first part of the question. 'They don't tell you everything, you know. I suppose he's come on business.' He stepped round to the other side of the car, his head tilted as if he were admiring it. He noticed the immaculately-clean tyres, the wheel jack and the wet stiff-bristled brush which were lying to one side. 'Anyway,' he added, 'I don't want to hinder you, mate. I'll leave you to it.'

He walked away, back to Spratt's car, banging the door when he got in just to let the big man know where he was.

Spratt reappeared some ten minutes later. 'I didn't get much,' he grunted as he settled into the driving seat and started the engine. 'What about you?'

'The car's being washed,' Garrett replied as they moved smoothly down the drive. 'Very thoroughly, too. Especially the tyres, the treads have been scrubbed out with a brush and water. Now that's a thing the normal car owner doesn't do.'

'Ah! Mr. Dykes will be interested in that. I took the line that a man had been reported as having been seen to leave the grounds in a hurry last night — which Read probably did — so we, the police, were checking Pelford had suffered no loss from an intruder.' He turned left towards Whitsea. 'Pelford assured me nowhere had been broken into, nothing was missing. But he was obviously wary, and, I thought, more than a little on edge. And another thing, he didn't — What's up?'

Garrett had twisted quickly round in his seat to stare through the rear window. For some seconds he didn't reply to Spratt's question. Then he turned forward again.

'We've just met Molly Bilton in her car,' he said. 'And she's turned into Pelford's place. That's interesting, too. Sorry, sir, I interrupted you.'

'I was just saying that Pelford didn't ask why an inspector had come on such a trifling routine enquiry. As a former con, he'll know all about police rank, and the normal duties attached to each, no doubt. Pelford was certainly playing it very cagily. There's something queer there, Dick. I'd bet my pension on it.'

'Did you mention Mrs. Graham, sir?'

'I did, using the 'I believe you had a visit, etc.' line. He didn't seem surprised at that question, either. I had the impression he had an answer ready for it. Mrs. Graham, from the Palladium, is a friend of his receptionist, Miss Henson, I was told. She visits Miss Henson now and then when her evening duties in the box-office are over.

'To sum it all up, I think we can tell Mr. Dykes we've put Pelford in Uneasy Street. If he has any jobs in prospect here, he'll think twice before doing them now, I fancy. 'Crime prevention is a basic duty of all branches of the police.' I quote — you know the Manual. We may not have done much good this morning, but at least we've done no harm.'

16

Molly Bilton had not seen Garrett and Spratt. That part of her mind not taken up by driving was busy weighing up the pros and cons of the news Dennis Read had telephoned to her. On her previous visit to Healthways Martin Pelford had been definitely unco-operative. This hadn't worried Molly particularly, her own plans could proceed without Pelford's help, and she knew where she was, having plumbed Pelford's attitude. But there was the tape recording Pelford had made of their conversation. Molly wanted that back. She thought, after Pelford had heard what she had to say this morning, that he would hand it over readily enough.

She parked her car by the front steps of Healthways and rang the bell. Gaye Henson, who answered it, stared at the caller with unveiled hostility.

'Yes? What is it?' She planted herself

directly in the doorway as if she were prepared to resist any physical invasion Molly was likely to make.

'Mr. Pelford. I wish to see him, at once.'

'Mr. Pelford is particularly busy this morning. And he's already been hindered by visitors.'

'All the same, you will kindly tell him Miss Bilton is here.' Her voice hardened. 'You will be sorry if you don't, I assure you.'

'Oh, very well!' Gaye flounced away, leaving Molly on the steps. She was back within thirty seconds.

'Mr. Pelford will see you.' She was still sulky, mutinous. Molly smiled at her sweetly, stepped past her into the hall. 'He's in his office — you know where that is.' She went quickly away.

Molly walked into Pelford's office without knocking. Pelford looked up from behind his desk and gave her a wintry smile.

'Ah, Miss Bilton again. Find yourself a chair. It's fortunate you called, I was contemplating getting in touch with you myself.' He took off his heavy glasses, peered closely at her, replaced the glasses.

'What about?' If abruptness was the game, Molly could play that with anyone.

'Last night a man was trying to spy on us here. I regret to say he escaped before we could apprehend him. One of your employees, wasn't it?'

'What makes you think that?'

Pelford shrugged. 'It appears obvious to me. I have something you would like to acquire. Let me tell you, however, that any efforts in that direction are fore-doomed failures.'

'I happen to know the police are interested in you. This man could have been a plainclothes jack. He was probably trying to discover whether Ray Lever was still in hiding here.'

Pelford frowned, as if trying to catch a recollection.

'Lever . . . Ah, I remember. On your last visit you mentioned that name. I told you then I knew nothing about such a person. Must I repeat this?'

'You're wasting you breath if you do. Anyway, Lever isn't important any more. He's dead.'

Her eyes concentrated on Pelford's face, but it showed no particular reaction. He shrugged again.

'Am I expected to express condolences? These would hardly be sincere, since I never knew the fellow.'

'I told you Lever was in my employ. He was found dead, strangled, in a shed near Whitsea this morning. The police noticed he resembled the man wanted for a shooting on the caravan site. He has been identified by Kendall, the man he shot at. It was found he had a record, which the police will have by now.'

'I don't see how all this concerns me, Miss Bilton. Yet you must think it does, or you would not be here.'

'I'll tell you how it concerns you, Mr. Martin Pelford,' Molly said quietly. She began to talk, still quietly.

Pelford listened, without moving a muscle, though before she had finished there were beads of sweat on his forehead. He took out a handkerchief and wiped his face.

'You haven't the least shred of proof,'

he said. 'It would be your word against mine, if it came to the — er — crunch.'

Molly smiled. 'You're talking rubbish, you know. Lever was here, and once the police know that, they'll be on to you like a ton of bricks. When they really turn on the heat, I know at least two people who will sing.' She held out a slender hand with the fingers crooked. 'So, gimme.'

Pelford said, 'Perhaps. And all in good time.' He was looking at her with curiosity now. 'If Lever is dead, that must seriously affect your own plans. What are you going to do, now you haven't a peterman?'

'I can find a substitute. Not one in Lever's class, I admit, but one who'll do the job I have in mind. But it does leave me with a man short, and here we might get together, don't you think?'

'I am not interested, Miss Bilton. Please take that as being very definite, and my last word.'

'Please yourself. I'll manage somehow. I don't intend to go away from Whitsea empty-handed. Now may I have that tape recording?'

'In a moment. Meanwhile, I'm curious. You mentioned two persons who would, as you put it, sing under pressure. Who are these people?'

'As if you didn't know! Puffer Tenby is one and the woman from the Palladium box-office is the other. I think Graham is her name. She was visiting here last night.'

Pelford allowed himself a chuckle. 'Your man, the one who was snooping around here, probably saw her. She came to see my receptionist, Miss Henson, with whom she is friendly. I deduce your man telephoned the police, anonymously, with the information. I've had one of them here this morning, doing what I believe is termed a follow-up. He was quite satisfied with my explanation. And why not, since it is the truth?'

Molly said, 'You've promised to hand over that tape recording. Why? It was useful to you when you made it, wasn't it? What's happened to change your mind?'

Pelford leaned back in his chair.

'It is really none of your business, Miss

Bilton, but it so happens that I have had to face the fact that Healthways, as a commercial venture, is not proving successful. I intend to close down here soon.'

'Really? The cops must have put a proper scare into you! But, as you say, it's no concern of mine. So if you'll let me have that tape, I'll be on my way.'

Pelford pressed his desk bell, Gaye Henson answered it, she was requested to bring the tape recorder. Neither Molly nor Pelford had anything to say to each other while they waited.

The machine was carried in by Gaye. She was thanked and dismissed. Pelford unlocked the case, lifted its lid and set the spools running in reverse. Molly had risen to her feet and was watching closely. When the tape had run off, Pelford put out his hand to remove the spool, but Molly stopped him.

'Just a minute. Play it back. I want to check it's the right one.'

Pelford's heavy brows lifted. 'At least, Miss Bilton, you could have done me the honour to trust me. However, as you wish.' He set the spools running forward and Molly, with her head on one side, listened carefully to her voice, and Pelford's, as their previous conversation, during which Molly had admitted her unlawful intentions, poured out of the speaker.

'You wouldn't have been crafty enough to have made a duplicate of that lot?' she queried as Pelford ran the spools in reverse.

'The answer to that is no,' he replied with some asperity. 'You may not believe that, but it happens to be true.' He handed the tape to her. 'We have nothing more to say to each other, I think.'

'Except to say good morning.' Molly flashed him a brilliant smile as she turned towards the door. 'I'll let myself out.'

She went back to her car and started it up. None of the information she had picked up that morning suggested any major change in her original plans. At a pinch, Denny Read could stand in for Lever. She'd talk to the gang this afternoon, but she wouldn't mention that tape-recording. She had slipped up there, giving Pelford the chance to make it, and it didn't do for a leader to confess she'd boobed as badly as that.

17

Detective Superintendent Welling, seated at the head of the table in his room at Whitsea Central, looked around with an air of some complacency. As on the previous Sunday morning, Spratt and Garrett, Dykes and Prior were all present.

'I am a man,' Welling said, 'who gives credit where credit is due. Therefore, I see no reason why I shouldn't take credit when I have earned it. You will all remember that when we gathered here before, I gave it as my opinion there were two gangs, and not one, working here. Events seem to be proving me correct.'

Dykes said blandly, 'We certainly are coming to the conclusion that Pelford and his crowd are up to no good, sir, and the Molly Bilton lot are acting queerly, too. But the robberies which have worried us all took place before Bilton and her friends appeared.'

'Before we *knew* they were on our

patch, inspector,' Welling corrected him. 'Your point is a minor one and doesn't affect the main issue.'

Dykes let it go with shrug. 'It's Lever's killing which is bothering me at the moment. No hard evidence anywhere. We've identified him and that's about all. Forensic has been particularly unhelpful — mind, I'm not blaming them. You can't find what isn't there. Ockley, the lad from Faynor, is fairly sure it was a Saab he saw parked by the field gate, and Pelford owns one — which was thoroughly cleaned before we could get to it. Sergeant Garrett here noticed the car had Goodyear tyres, and the tracks to the shed match up with that, but it's a widely-used make and I don't think we can get much there.'

'But you're still suspicious of that Healthways lot?'

'Young Colin Taylor was sure he'd seen a man answering to Lever's description at Healthways,' Dykes reminded his superior. 'Lever could have gone to earth there after he'd shot Kendall in the caravan.'

'But Garrett got mixed up with that

shooting on the cliff the same night,' Welling said. 'That's a hell of a long step from Healthways, if it was Lever again.'

'I'd be inclined to doubt it was,' Spratt put in. 'The whole incident is pointless. Why pull a gun on a courting couple like that? Unless it was the husband of the woman that fellow — what was his name? — was with.'

'Theaker, sir,' Prior supplied. 'And I checked that point. Made Theaker tell me who she was. Her husband was in the hotel playing cards with a party the whole evening.'

'I followed Read from the caravan site on to those cliffs,' Garrett added. 'He could have done the shooting, though I don't see why he should.'

'Let's leave it, and the murder job, for the moment,' Welling said. 'Let's have a round-up of all the other bits and pieces. I understand they've been channelled to you, inspector. What do they all add up to?'

Spratt leaned back in his chair. 'We've got these two characters, Beryl Graham and Puffer Tenby. Tenby is, or has been, one of Sergeant Prior's most valued snouts. He's passed word of a possible bank robbery, which has been covered as far as possible in case the information is genuine. But we know he's in contact with Molly Bilton, and Molly is tied up with the Reads and Kendalls. None of you need any reminder from me that the grasser, the snout, will play both sides against the middle if it suits his book. It happens all the time.

'Beryl Graham visited Healthways last night. Pelford says she's a friend of his receptionist, but according to what young Taylor heard, she wasn't welcome there.'

'Seems to me,' Welling grunted, 'you people are depending a lot on this lad's stories.'

Spratt nodded. 'We've got to use the pinch of salt here, I agree. But the boy seems sensible enough and we can't afford to miss any tricks. You'll accept, sir, that the Palladium affair smells of collusion?'

Welling nodded. 'I'll give you that.'

'Molly Bilton also paid a visit to Healthways this morning. Pelford knew her father in jail. I have a very strong feeling that Molly was out to suggest an amalgamation. Either that, or to warn Pelford off any territory she herself has an eye on.'

'So,' Welling said, 'we've talked it all over. Now it's time we did something. What d'you suggest, inspector?'

'I realise Mr. Dykes and his lads have their hands full with this killing, sir. That job's priority, of course. But Tenby certainly needs watching, and Sergeant Garrett, I'm sure, will have another look at that gentleman for you this evening.'

Garrett nodded. 'Leave it to me, sir.'

'Of course,' Spratt went on, 'Tenby and Mrs. Graham will have to be pulled in soon and leaned on a bit. I hardly feel this is the moment, though. What do you say, Mr. Welling?'

The superintendent made a show of deep consideration.

'Probably not. The great thing in circumstances like these is to know just when to move in. Too soon — too late — and you spoil everything. Like — er — '

'Like the cymbals coming in wrong in an orchestral piece, sir?' Prior suggested helpfully.

Welling looked at him. 'Something of the sort. The essential thing now is to get some of these loose ends tied up.'

And, Garrett thought some four hours later, I've got myself nicely tied up, too. It was crazy, really. He was at Whitsea to convalesce, to take it easy, to get himself fit for an early return to work. Yet here he was, in the Blue Lion again, spinning out a pint of beer while he waited for Puffer Tenby to show up, for all the world as if he were back on duty at Deniston.

He smiled to himself. He was enjoying it all; the last few days had, at least, done him some mental good. A bored convalescent never made much progress. The doctors had a sound line when they recommended occupational therapy.

It was at this stage of his reflections when he seized his glass hurriedly and lifted it to shield his face. A big wide-shouldered man had just come in and Garrett recognised him as the fellow who had been washing the red Saab so thoroughly, the fellow who had pitched into Colin Taylor. Ah — Canning! That was the name Colin had mentioned.

The Blue Lion was not yet at its busiest and Garrett had been able to choose a secluded corner near the door. Canning went to the bar, looking about him. His back was towards Garrett now, and the C.I.D. man was comfortably certain he hadn't been seen. He picked up the evening paper he had brought with him and bent over it.

Canning ordered a half of bitter and stood sipping it. Several minutes ticked by and then Puffer Tenby appeared. Garrett saw Canning's head jerk up. He raised a hand to Puffer, who angled across the room to a small empty table. Canning finished his drink quickly and gave another order. When he turned away from the bar he was carrying a glass of whisky — a double — in one hand, and a half pint of bitter in the other. He sat down at Puffer's table, pushing the whisky across to him.

Puffer picked up the whisky and took it down in two quick swallows. He wiped his mouth with the back of his hand and grinned. Canning at once got up and returned to the bar to repeat the spirits order.

For the next half hour Puffer downed the succession of whiskies Canning brought him while Canning himself merely played with his beer. It was obvious to Garrett that Canning was out to get his companion drunk. He seemed to be succeeding, judging by the fixed, foolish grin which had appeared on the little man's face, and by the unco-ordinated efforts he made to pick up his glass. The two didn't talk much. Puffer was inclined to be loquacious but Canning did his best to keep him quiet.

Busy as he was, the barman was keeping an eye on Puffer, and at last he shook his head when Canning again put the whisky glass on the counter. The man in the white jacket had decided Puffer had had enough and he wasn't going to serve him again. Canning shrugged, turned away and went back to the little man. By his gestures he seemed to be urging Puffer outside, but Puffer, still smiling stupidly, was apparently quite happy where he was. Canning's face lost its amiability. He leant over Puffer and grabbed one of his arms, sinking his fingers hard into the triceps muscle. Puffer's grin was suddenly replaced by a scowl as he tried to wrench his arm free. Canning let him go, began to talk to him. With one of the sudden changes of mind typical of a drunken man, Puffer nodded in quite a friendly manner and got unsteadily to his feet. Canning guided him to the door. Garrett folded up his paper and followed the pair outside.

Still aided by Canning, Puffer was making a stumbling progress across the foreshore road to the opposite pavement, where iron railings topped the low wall which separated the road from the beach. Having reached the railings, Puffer seemed inclined to let them support him but Canning urged him on. Puffer nodded solemnly several times, heaved himself upright and moved towards the harbour. Garrett also crossed the road and followed.

The ill-assorted pair passed the lifeboat

station and turned on to a concrete walk which took them to the huge open-fronted shed where, in the early mornings, the fish auctions took place. Wooden steps at each end gave access to a railed gallery off which were situated the various offices and storerooms necessary to Whitsea's fishing industry. Garrett moved along the quay until, between the funnels and deckhouses of two of the moored trawlers, he had a view into the shed. He saw Puffer mount the steps at the far end, and, after some fumbling, produce a key. Canning snatched it from him and opened the door of one of the offices. He shoved Puffer inside, took the key out of the lock, and followed him in.

Garrett moved quickly. He dodged back along the quay and gained the shed. He went quietly up the steps opposite to those the pair had used and began to walk along the gallery. At intervals, alongside the series of doors. fish-boxes were standing in high, neat stacks. Garrett grinned with satisfaction. The stack by the door which his quarry had entered would prove excellent cover. He hoped the wooden walls weren't thick enough to prevent him from hearing what was going on inside.

He positioned himself, and at once heard voices. Canning's first, he seemed to be conducting the proceedings, with some authority in his tone, too.

'Now we're here with nobody listening,' he said, 'your job is to pull yourself together, my friend. I'm going to ask you a few questions and I want the right answers, don't forget.'

There was a short interval of silence and then Puffer asked, 'What'sh you wanna know, then?'

'Listen. Last night you met a man called Kendall in the pub. We know this for a fact. After you'd talked to him you went to that amusement place and played the pintables. Correct?'

'Lotsa fellers talk to me in the Lion. Well-known char'ter, me. Look, pal, I tellya — '

'You tell me what the woman and you were talking about by the pin-table. You know who I mean, her name's Bilton.'

'Bil'on . . . See, pal, I never saw this

dame before lasht night. Crossh me heart, I never d'nt. She just says how'm I doing and like that, see.' He cackled hoarsely. 'Ships wot pass in night, tha's all.'

'Don't give me that. You were watched. Kendall told you where to meet up with her, didn't he? Didn't he?'

The repetition of the question was accompanied by the slurring of footsteps on the wooden floor, as if, Garrett thought, Canning had moved closer to Puffer, was no doubt standing over him, with menacing fists.

'All ri'. No need to . . . ' There was alarm in Puffer's voice now. 'But you got it all wrong, y'know. This chap in the Lion — wha' say's name was? — we was jus' chatting casual, like. I meantersay, I fell over his foot what was stuck out an' he bought me a beer. 'Sall. Look, mate, what we come here for anyway? You tell me you wanna talk privit and me, I finds you a nice place and now it's all queshsuns and sorta threats.' A whine came into his voice. 'An' you won' believe me when I'm shpeaking truth!'

'Okay.' Footsteps again, but these were

more distinct and regular, as if Canning had begun to pace the floor. 'Now, listen. A fellow was killed, strangled, in a shed not far from here last night. It's in the evening paper.'

'Well, I di'n't do it and I don't read the papers.'

'Cut out the cracks and listen, like I said. Last night we had a fellow snooping around our place. But you'd know about that, wouldn't you?'

'Me? What the hell, mate? I dunno what you're on about.'

'You're in with this Bilton lot, Tenby, and it was one of them who was doing the snooping.'

'I've jus' tole you — '

'I know you have, and I don't believe you. Let's get on. We weren't able to nail this chap but I reckon he didn't scarper altogether. He hung around somewhere and then, later on, he pinched my boss's car. Why, when he had a car of his own? The answer's easy, if you remember that man who was killed. You're with me?'

'I c'd do with another drink,' Puffer said. 'Clear me brain, it would.'

'You can't have one just now. I'm telling you I've good reason to think this fellow used Mr. Pelford's car to dump that body in the shed.'

'But you jus' said he had a car, didn't you?'

'I did. But he didn't want his own spotted, see? Or to have the cops finding clues in it. That's how I figure it.'

'Where's this car now, then, the one what he used?'

'Back in the garage. You see, he returned it when he'd done with it. But I reckon it must have been seen, because a couple of cops came round today and one of 'em seemed very interested in the car.'

'You mean — looking for clues and that?'

'He was just looking, but I could tell. I was washing the car at the time. Gave it a right do, and all.'

'You shouldn' done it.' Puffer's voice was solemn. 'Destroying ev'dence — s'not right.'

'Look mate, here's the point. He — this Bilton gang bloke — couldn't have taken that car if I hadn't left the keys in it.'

'Lef' the keys? What you do that for?'

'Because I forgot 'em when I put the car away.'

Canning was beginning to sound impatient. 'And if my boss knew that, I'd be in most hellish trouble. He won't stand for such carelessness — if he found out I'd be for it proper.'

'So what? And why're you telling me all this?'

'Because, as we all know, you've got the ear of the cops. You could whisper — and you're going to — that the killing was done by Bilton's people. Which it was. Oh, I know it's possible the whole story'll have to come out, about me leaving the keys in the car, and so on, but then again, it mightn't. I mean, when the cops are put on to the right people, and they find out the truth, I might still manage to keep in the clear. I don't want to lose my job.'

'And why should I tell the rozzers an'thing about it?'

'Because . . . Look, here's five to be going on with. Five more when you've done what I say.'

'Gimme the ten now, an' I will.'

'I haven't that much on me. Go on, take these. That's fixed, then. Now, let's get on to the main issue. Bilton and her mob have got a big job planned here — right? And you're helping them. So we want to know all about it. Start talking, Tenby!'

'You got it all wrong. I know nothin' about these people you're on about — '

The crack of the shot, the buzz of the bullet past his head and its clunking thud into the door all seemed simultaneous to Garrett. Instinctively he threw himself forward and sideways, straight at the edge of the pile of fish-boxes. In a series of deafening crashes, they collapsed over and around him, sliding in a cascade down the wooden steps to the concrete floor of the shed.

The office door was wrenched open as he struggled to free himself, and, at the same time, to keep on his feet. He had a glimpse of Puffer standing, open-mouthed, in the doorway. The unseen gunman loosed off another shot. Puffer let out a yell of alarm and flung himself flat on the floor. As Garrett was still trying to fend off the falling boxes, Canning came out like a bull at a gate. He leapt over Puffer, took the steps in two bounds and went charging out of the shed. At the same moment Garrett tripped and fell helplessly forward. The edge of one of the boxes slammed into his damaged thigh. Pain seared him like a white-hot flame. He managed to shove the box away and then he was fighting a red mist before his eyes, a roaring in his ears, and he struggled not to faint.

Long minutes seemed to pass as he lay there, teeth gritted, fingernails digging into palms, waiting grimly for the worst of the agony to subside. The effort brought the sweat out all over his body, underlying his physical torment was the fear that his fall had opened up the deep gash in his thigh. He had no room in his mind for Puffer, for Canning, for the man who had been shooting . . .

Pain began to dull, his heart steadied. Slowly, he got to his feet. One hand, fearing what it might find, went to the site of his wound. There was no wet, spreading patch on the outside of his flannel slacks. He heaved a quick sigh of relief, loosed his belt and made a closer, next-to-the-skin exploration. The surgeons had done a good job. The scar tissue was intact, there was no serious damage. He grinned to himself as his fears evaporated. The leg was hurting like Hades, but that would wear off.

He picked a way through the scattered boxes and limped into the room Puffer and Canning had used. It was empty now and recollection came to him that, while he was writhing in pain, he had heard a second set of footsteps go down from the gallery. Puffer had obviously picked himself up and cleared off, without bothering to lock up the office. The key was still in the lock on the inside of the door.

Garrett looked around, examining the place by the aid of the single, unshaded light bulb which dangled from the ceiling. It seemed to be the office of one of the smaller firms which dealt with the catches the trawlers brought in. But it had a telephone, as Garrett had hoped. The instrument was on the window sill.

He rang Whitsea Central and asked for C.I.D. The detective on stand-by duty took his call. Garrett reported briefly — a gunman on the loose, Tenby and Canning involved in the incident. The duty man promised to get in touch with Inspector Dykes at once. Garrett thanked him, slapped dust from the local directory on which the telephone was standing and looked up the number of Spratt's hotel. He was promised the inspector would be paged at once and, in fact, Spratt was on the line within two minutes.

'You're sure you've not really damaged yourself, Dick?' he asked when he had heard Garrett's story. 'Good. Hang on where you are and I'll come down and pick you up.'

Garrett put the receiver down. There were two wooden chairs in the office. One of them looked fairly comfortable. But before he lowered himself into it, he took out his pocketknife and dug the flattened bullet out of the door.

Once a policeman, always a policeman, he thought, and smiled wryly as he wrapped his trophy in a clean handkerchief.

18

It was a quarter to ten that evening when Spratt and Garrett turned in to Whitsea Central. They were taken to Dykes' room at once.

'We haven't picked up that gunman yet,' he told them. 'There was a patrol car at the harbour within minutes of the report. They couldn't find the gunman, nor Tenby, nor Canning. Nor anyone who had seen them. There are few people around there at this time of night.'

Garrett produced his handkerchief-wrapped bullet and laid it on the desk in front of Dykes. The inspector nodded.

'From a Walther P38,' he said. 'Our chaps found a couple of ejected shells in that shed. We identified them from the firing pin and ejector claw marks without any trouble. The devil of it is, we've neither bullets nor shells from the other two shootings, the one on the caravan site and the other on the cliffs, so we can't say the same gun was used for all three.'

'Awkward,' Spratt commented, 'when you thought you had the gunman on a morgue slab, with the tab of Ray Lever round his neck.'

'Yes.' Dykes frowned. 'Yet the dead man there matches up with his C.R.O. details, you know, even if Kendall wasn't a hundred per cent sure about him. My guess is that whoever croaked Lever took his gun. And even if he hadn't any spare ammo, a Walther fires eight at a loading, you know. The present holder of it could still have four shots left.'

'There was no cartridge case found in the Kendalls' van, was there, sir?' Garrett asked. 'So if it was the same gun, where did that go to?'

'An interesting problem, sergeant,' Dykes said. 'But one we can put aside at the moment. Let's have an account of your adventures.'

Garrett gave it. At its conclusion Dykes nodded and said, 'So much for the facts. Now let's have your comments.'

'Well, sir, in the first place I'm sure Puffer wasn't as plastered as he pretended to be. He knocked a few whiskies back, that's for sure, but I thought he was overdoing the drunk act. Of course, I don't know his capacity.'

'He's got the best head for liquor between Flamborough and Tynemouth,' Prior, who had joined them during Garrett's recital, averred. 'If, as it seems to me, Canning was trying to get him tight so he'd open up and talk plenty, the said Canning was on a loser.'

'Puffer certainly wasn't giving anything away about Molly Bilton and her pals,' Garrett agreed. 'At least, not up to the moment the shot was fired. And what about Canning's story of the Saab being taken from Healthways? If it's true, Read must have done that.'

'If it's true,' Dykes repeated. He turned to Spratt. 'I'm having Tenby looked for and brought in. Mrs. Graham, too, as soon as she's free this evening. But I have the feeling Canning can wait till morning. What do you think?'

'I'd say that's sound timing. Those two both have a few questions to answer and you can often get at the big shots by wading into the little ones first. You want to interview Tenby on his own?'

'I fancy we'd get more out of him if he's faced by the whole crowd of us here. Between us, we should be able to sort him out, I think. See if there's any news of him, will you, Prior?'

Prior went out, but he was back almost at once, shoving Puffer Tenby's small wizened figure before him.

'Just been brought in, sir.' He placed a chair and nodded the little man into it. Puffer blinked as he stared around.

'What's all this about, then?' he demanded. 'Me, I'm just on me way to bed when this patrol car rolls up and nothing'll do but I get dragged here. What's the idea?'

Dykes leaned forward. 'You've got us a trifle worried, Puffer. You told Sergeant Prior a few days ago that a bank hold-up was being planned on our patch here. Your information is usually accurate, so, of course, we've taken precautions. But no job of that sort has been attempted yet. So we've asked you to come in and give us a few more details.'

Puffer rubbed his hands down the sides of his trousers.

'That's somethin' I can't do, Mr. Dykes. It was just what I happened to hear in a pub. There was these two fellers, see. Londoners, by their talk. Visitors they looked like. One was saying there'd be plenty of money in the Whitsea banks at the eight of the season and his mate said sure and how about knockin' one or two of 'em off? Then they saw me listening and got up and went out. Never seen 'em since. Only I thought it best to tell Mr. Prior here.'

'Can you describe these men?'

Puffer dry-shaved his jaw. 'Ordinary sort of blokes, they was. One was fair and the other dark. Sports clothes, no hats.'

'In other words,' Dykes said sharply, 'you needed an easy quid, so you made up this tale of a bank robbery and told it to Sergeant Prior.'

'Now, look, Mr. Dykes! You got me all wrong — '

'What have you been doing with yourself this evening?'

'Well, I — er — ' He became aware of

himself as the focus of four pairs of staring eyes, and swallowed hard.' I've bin to the Lion, and had a couple of drinks, that's all.'

'You met a man named Canning there, by appointment.' Spratt spoke for the first time since Puffer had entered. The small man turned his head to look him up and down.

'And 'oo might you be, mister?'

'Detective Inspector Spratt, North Central Crime Squad,' he was told crisply. 'And while we're at it, this is my associate, Detective Sergeant Garrett. Now tell us what Canning and you talked about.'

'Look!' Puffer threw up his hands. 'You got it all wrong. I was talking to a bloke there. He bought me a few drinks. But I met him by chance, like — '

'You were watched,' Spratt said harshly. 'Last night, too. You met Kendall then, who told you where you could have a talk to Molly Bilton. Now you'd better open up and tell us what you know. And when you do, it'll be checked. remember that!'

'Well, I'll go to 'ell!' Puffer exuded

indignation. 'Me, I'm a respect'ble citizen, and I've helped the police because I knows where me duty lies and all the thanks I get — '

It was Dykes who broke in this time.

'You were shot at tonight, Puffer. Shot at twice. They're out to get you — you know that? And next time they mightn't miss.'

Puffer wiped a dirty hand across his face without making a reply. The internal communications box on the table buzzed. Dykes pressed a key. 'Yes?'

'The other person has been brought in, sir,' a disembodied voice said.

'Thanks.' Dykes nodded to Prior. 'Take this man to the interrogation room, sergeant. We'll talk to him again later. Then you can bring our second visitor in.'

'It's Beryl Graham,' he said when Prior and Puffer had gone. 'I've known her since schooldays, and I'm afraid she's not apt to accord my rank much respect.' He grinned at Spratt.

'Right, I'll tackle her,' Spratt responded. 'Tough case, eh?'

'She'll have plenty to say — and we've

no real evidence against her. In that line we'll only get what she provides us with herself.'

Spratt nodded. When Beryl Graham was brought in by Prior, the little group rearranged itself. Spratt was now in the big chair, with Dykes at his side and a little to the rear. Garrett had slid his seat towards a corner, and the chair Puffer had used was placed squarely in front of the table, under the main lighting strip. At a nod from Dykes, Prior remained standing with his back to the door when he had ushered Beryl into her seat. Beryl patted at her dyed hair, staring at them in turn. She took in a long breath, but before she could utter a word, Spratt was talking.

'Mrs. Graham, I am Detective Inspector Spratt from Deniston. You have been asked to come here because we wish you to answer some questions.'

'Look, mister. I've told you lot over and over about what happened at the Palladium Sat'day night. I'm fed-up of talking about it. I've wrote it all out and signed it. So what more?'

'We aren't concerned at the moment with the incident you refer to, madam. A man was done to death last night in a shed just off the Faynor Road. No doubt you will have seen the newspaper report.'

'I have, but what it's got to do with me I wouldn't know. I didn't kill the feller. I'll write that down, and sign it, if it'll make you happy. Then p'raps I can be on me way home. I've had a hard day and it's late.'

'The last thing we imagine is that you were concerned in this homicide, Mrs. Graham. But you may be able to help us in another way. You visited the Healthways Guest House late yesterday evening, I believe?'

The woman stared at him, her aggressive self-confidence suddenly gone.

'Come along, Mrs. Graham,' Spratt urged. 'We're not here to waste time. Answer my question, please.'

'And what if I did? What's it got to do with you?'

'Why did you go there? Why did Mr. Canning, whom you met at the gate, tell you you shouldn't have come at all?'

'Because — Because it was getting a bit late, see? A bit late for visiting, like.'

'And who were you visiting there?'

'I — I wanted to see Mr. Pelford on a private matter.'

'You must tell us what that matter was, Mrs. Graham.'

'Well, you see ... Well, a friend of mine's coming to Whitsea soon, on holiday, like, and I'm trying to find her somewhere to stay. And I thought Mr. Pelford's place 'ud just suit her, so I went to see if he could put her up.'

'You'll have to think of a better story than that, before I believe you, Mrs. Graham.'

Spratt had deliberately prodded her to the point where her self-control vanished. She sprang from her chair, swinging round on Dykes, preferring to wreak her rage on him rather than on this stranger with the grim voice and the probing, inquisitorial manner.

'What is all this, Charlie Dykes? You've no right to have me brought here to be badgered like this! And I'll tell you something else, an' all! I'm not saying another word, to any of you!'

Dykes sent a glance past her to Spratt, a silent question to which an unspoken answer was made.

'Fair enough, Beryl,' Dykes said cheerfully. 'Nobody wants to rush you. You aren't all that important at the moment. Of course, if I'd been in your place, I wouldn't have let them take it all. I'd have kept some back, to make sure I did get my cut.'

The woman's face flamed. 'I dunno what you're on about.'

'See Mrs. Graham out, will you, Sergeant Prior?' Dykes went on. 'We'll be watching her house, so she won't go far away. And bring Puffer Tenby in again on your way back, please.'

'You got him here?' Beryl shouted. 'And what's he bin saying, the scraped-down little bastard? If you believe him, you'll believe anything! I'm telling you — '

'Goodnight, Beryl,' Dykes said calmly. 'We'll be seeing you again.' She turned and cursed him roundly as Prior led her firmly out.

'She'll break,' Spratt said with a grin as the door closed. 'You just need that little bit of hard evidence to hit her with. It'll come. Do you want me to carry on with Tenby?'

'If you would.' Dykes looked at his watch. 'It's getting late, and we've no legal right to hold him here much longer. I certainly hope . . . '

Spratt nodded. 'Leave it to me.'

Puffer was still inclined to be indignant. 'There's nowt more I can tell you,' he said when he was ushered in, 'so it's no use going on at me. And I want to get home to me bed.'

'That's just the trouble, Mr. Tenby,' Spratt told him. 'We can send you home in a police car, but we can't guarantee to protect you once you're there. There just isn't the staff available.'

'What you mean — protect?'

'You've been shot at once — twice, actually — tonight. If, as it seems, this crazy gunman has it in for you, he's not going to give up in a hurry. For all we know, he's hanging about outside now, waiting to get you before you can step

290

into the car. Or he may be actually hiding in the vicinity of your house. So until we can put him under lock and key ... ' Spratt shrugged.

Sweat had broken out on Puffer's face. 'What 'ud anybody want to do me for?'

'I think you can work that out if you try. Maybe you have some information which somebody else is anxious you shouldn't pass on. Perhaps someone suspects you of doing a double-cross and is out to prevent it. Did you have any sort of a view of the man who shot at you?'

'Not of his face, I didn't. But I saw the back of him when he run off. He was shortish, thin and — yes, that's right — his ears stuck out. He wasn't wearing no hat, you see.'

'We'll try to find him,' Spratt said. 'The Whitsea police on patrol have been alerted already, of course, but with no sort of description they haven't had much chance of picking him up. Now you have given us something to work on. There's a car waiting to take you home. Goodnight.'

'Couldn't I stay 'ere for the night, where it's safe?' Puffer appealed to Dykes.

'That's not possible, Puffer. You'll have to take a chance. After all, you got yourself into this. Go home and think about that fact, and we'll have another talk tomorrow.'

When he returned from seeing Puffer out, Prior reported, 'Canning's safely back at Healthways, sir. I sent young Herries to keep an eye on that place, and he's just rung in.'

'Good,' Dykes responded. 'You know, I think Puffer wasn't pulling anything when he described that gunman at the harbour. Short and thin with outstanding ears. It's not much, though.'

'Read, at the caravan site,' Garrett said suddenly. 'The description fits him exactly. And I'm willing to bet tonight's not the first time he's used that gun.'

'You mean,' Spratt said, 'on the cliffs the other night? Yes, you could be right at that. Though I can't see any reason for such an act, not yet, at any rate.'

Dykes' hand went to his intercom. The desk sergeant's voice replied to the pressed key.

'Get me Grinstead, the warden at the

Northway Road caravan site, please,' Dykes requested.

They waited, without speaking, their eyes on the telephone, like sprinters in their blocks tensed for the gun. Then the bell shrilled and Dykes snatched up the receiver.

'Mr. Grinstead? Inspector Dykes here. I'm just checking on those two families you have there — the Reads and the Kendalls. They're still with you? . . . What's that? . . . Just a moment, sir.' His left hand grabbed a pencil, and Prior slid a notepad to him. 'Right. All the details, please.'

He listened and scribbled. Then, 'Thanks very much, Mr. Grinstead. Most helpful . . . Yes, I'll be in touch.'

He put the receiver down. 'Now we're starting to get action. Both those vans pulled out less than an hour ago.' He flicked the pad across the table to Prior. 'All stations call, sergeant. They won't have got far. Bring in for questioning.'

'Yessir.' Prior picked up the pad and went out again.

'A bit of luck there,' Dykes told the two

Deniston men. 'It's a regulation that every caravan and car booking in at the site has details taken of makes and registration numbers. So that lot is on the run, eh? Interesting to see what they've to say for themselves when we get 'em.'

Spratt nodded at the telephone. 'You could also make a call to the Burleigh Hotel, couldn't you?'

'Ah, yes! Miss Bilton, of course.' Once again he asked for a number, once again the bell rang and he lifted the receiver. Spratt and Garrett exchanged winks, like men who already know the answer.

The conversation was brief, Dykes recradled the handset. 'She's gone, too. Checked out about the same time as the caravan people. No car details this time, though.'

'I can give you those.' Garrett pulled out a diary. 'I made a note, when I saw her car on the site, just out of curiosity.'

Dykes took the diary. 'I'll just go and see these are added to the A.S. call.'

'And I'd better get myself home,' Garrett said when he and Spratt were alone. He grimaced. 'The leg's beginning to tell me it needs a rest in bed, sir.'

Spratt stood up. 'I'll run you back. There's nothing more to be done tonight — Dykes is quite right to leave Canning until the morning, I think — and if I don't miss my guess, I'll be back in Deniston by this time tomorrow.'

★   ★   ★

Hayburn and Scarr, the two patrolmen who had received the report of the caravan site shooting the previous Saturday, had been changed over to night shift. Hayburn was driving, cruising gently along the trunk road which led westwards from Whitsea, when the call came over the car radio. His mate snatched up a pad, scribbled details and then turned to Hayburn with a grin.

'You can do one of your famous tight U-turns, Frank. We just passed one of these guys, pulling in to that lay-by.'

And so Dennis Read, his head inside the bonnet of his car, cursing softly to himself and wondering what was up with the damn thing, while his wife Barbara held a wavering and inadequate torch, jerked upright at her sudden exclamation and found two large, gently-smiling policemen regarding him.

'Mr. Read, isn't it?' one of them said. 'We met at the caravan site the other day. I shall have to ask you to accompany us to the police station at Whitsea.'

Barbara Read flung round upon him angrily.

'This is ridiculous! Do you realise we have a small boy asleep in the back of the car? And that . . . '

'Carry him into the van and look after him there, madam,' Hayburn advised. 'You'll be all right. We'll send somebody along to keep an eye on you — and that's a promise.'

19

Spratt and Garrett were just leaving the building when Scarr and Hayburn brought Read in. The man was expostulating angrily.

'It's not right for a woman to be stuck out there alone with a small child at this time of night! I shall see this is reported!'

'I've told you we'll have a policewoman with her in no time,' Hayburn said sharply. The three went on down the corridor. Simultaneously, Garrett and Spratt had pulled up. They looked at each other.

'As you say, that leg of yours needs a rest,' Spratt said, and he kept all expression out of his voice.

'But it's a funny thing,' Garrett rejoined. 'It's gone completely better all at once, sir. And I'm sure Mr. Dykes would be only too pleased if we . . . I'll get hold of a phone and ring my digs. They get a bit anxious if I'm not in to time.'

Dykes met their reappearance with a welcoming grin. Prior had just settled Read into a chair, and when Dykes introduced the Deniston men, Spratt, watching closely, saw a flash of apprehension in Read's eyes at the mention of that city.

'You, I believe, are from Leicester, Mr. Read,' he said casually.

'That's right.' He looked hard at Garrett. 'I've seen you before somewhere, haven't I?'

Garrett nodded. 'At the caravan site last Saturday. I was with Inspector Dykes. I was admiring your car, that new Triumph Herald. It has a Deniston registration, hasn't it? Like Mr. Kendall's Cortina.'

'I can explain that — ' Read stopped, began again. 'Look, I want to know why I've been brought here. My wife and son — '

'Are being looked after, sir,' Dykes assured him. 'You were having a bit of engine trouble, I believe. We'll take care of that for you, as well. But let's get down to business. Do you own, or have in your possession, a Walther P38 automatic pistol?'

'Good God, no!' Read jumped up, spreading his arms. 'Here you are — search me!'

'Not necessary, sir. You sit down again. I understand, from a witness, that you were on the fish pier by the harbour this evening about nine-thirty?'

He saw Read was definitely worried now, but the man made an effort to bluster.

'I've every right to know what all these questions are leading to. I haven't been charged, you're trying to trap me. I'm saying nothing.' His lips clamped firmly together.

Dykes sighed. 'I wish you wouldn't take it this way, sir. We're only trying to check on Puffer Tenby's story — that you were the man who shot at him down there tonight. You know Puffer — at least, your friends Kendall and Molly Bilton know him. As you've no doubt discovered, Puffer's a bit of a dodger. It's practically your word against his.'

Read forgot his vow of silence. 'How

d'you mean — practically?'

'Mr. Canning, from Healthways, was there also. We haven't talked to him yet, but if Puffer saw the man who shot at him, Canning would also see him. We've Puffer's description, which fits you. We'll have to see if Mr. Canning's agrees, won't we? Meanwhile, we're holding you here on suspicion. Since you won't talk to us, it's the only thing we can do. And we mustn't forget, of course, that the man who shot at Kendall in the caravan has been found dead — murdered.'

Read licked his lips. 'I've every right to get a solicitor.'

Dykes gestured at the telephone. 'It's all yours.'

'Yeh, but — I don't know who to get. I mean, not in Whitsea.' He rubbed his chin. 'Look, I'm in a hell of a spot. Whatever I say might get other people into trouble.'

'You mean the Kendalls and Miss Bilton? All of whom, like yourself, have cut and run tonight? We'll be gathering them in any moment now, but I'm afraid it won't be possible for you all to have a nice get-together to decide on what's the best story to tell. Unless you all tell the best story, which is the truth.'

Read considered this, while the seconds ticked by on the office clock. Then he started up in his chair.

'Look, I've done nothing really wrong. I mean — Aw, I dunno!'

Dykes said persuasively, 'I want to know where the gun is. Give me that information and we'll have your caravan towed back on to the site, you can spend the night there with your wife and boy — there'll be a police guard, I warn you — and we'll have another talk in the morning.' He glanced at Spratt, who nodded agreement. 'Then you can get yourself fixed up with a solicitor and all the rest of it. But we must know what's happened to that automatic!'

'Canning's got it. He chased me, took it from me. There are still four cartridges in it.'

'Where did you get the gun?'

'I picked it up when Ray Lever dropped it, on the floor, after he'd loosed off at Ivor Kendall.'

'And why did Canning take it?' Dykes shot out the question.

Read licked his lips again. 'So he could do me in. He was going to. He collared me and wrenched the gun away.' Read was almost gabbling now. 'Look, you might as well know, he tried to kill me. At least, I mean that was his idea. He said as much. But I managed to get away, kicked him in the knee and dodged round a heap of fishing gear, on to the main road. I got back to the site and' — he stopped to gulp — 'we decided we'd be safer if we all cleared out. And I'm telling you, that fellow Canning's a killer. A killer, I say!'

Spratt asked quietly, 'And why should he want to kill you?'

'Because of what I know.'

'And what do you know?'

The fire went out of Read, suddenly. 'I've told you enough for now. Too much, maybe.'

He was talking to four experienced police officers. Each one of them knew Read had sung his piece for that night. Dykes nodded to Prior.

'Take him out, please, sergeant. Hay-burn and Scarr can run him back to that lay-by. Scarr's a mechanical genius, tell him to get the Herald running if possible, then they can escort the van back to the site. Arrange for a guard there, after which you can stand by here.

'I'm going to get Canning,' he added when Read and Prior had gone. 'What about it, you two?'

'I'm with you,' Spratt said. 'Pelford's my meat so we might as well clean up tonight.' He looked doubtfully at Garrett, who grinned.

'Just try keeping me out of this, sir, and you'll have more trouble on your hands.'

Dykes returned the grin. 'Three are always better than two,' he responded.

Dykes halted his car just short of the Healthways drive gates. Detective Con-stable Herries stepped out of a garden opposite, where he had been using a beech hedge for concealment.

'Nothing doing since I last reported in, sir,' he told Dykes. 'When the big fellow came back, he went part-way up the drive, then came back and set both gates

303

open, like they are now.'

'We'll go up on foot, shall we?' Dykes looked at Spratt, who nodded. 'There's a back way in — we've just passed it — a sort of lane too narrow to take a car,' Dykes went on. 'You nip back and cover the house from that side, Herries. With luck, it shouldn't be a long job.'

Spratt and Garrett followed him up the drive, walking on one of its grass verges. The house was in darkness, except for one window on the ground floor to the right of the front door. From this, light showed in a rectangle through a flowered curtain.

'I suggest you and I go in,' Dykes said to Spratt. 'And Garrett can cover the terrace. There's a pair of French windows opening on to it, with a side door just beyond. Okay?'

The others murmured agreement and, short of the front door steps, Garrett moved off to the left. Side by side, the two inspectors walked up the steps.

'Hallo, front door's open,' Dykes commented. His hand went out to the bell push, but Spratt, catching the sound of a loud voice, pressed his arm quickly.

'Hold on,' he said, 'I think we'd better just step inside without announcing ourselves.'

The hall was dark. It smelt faintly of floor polish. A line of light showed under a door on their right. They moved towards it cautiously, hands outstretched, feet sliding forward to avoid any obstacles which might lie in their path. From behind the door came a harsh voice.

'You've talked enough, Pelford. I know what I'm doing. So fork out those car keys and chuck 'em on the table. And no crafty tricks, or Gaye gets it — for keeps!'

Pelford spoke, wearily, like a man watching all he has built up tumbling into the dust.

'Oh, you can have the keys, Bert. And much good may they do you! I thought, when I chose you, I'd got a man with brains as well as brawn. How wrong can you get? If you'd just face one fact — that Read simply daren't talk. Don't you see he'd be — '

'The keys, damn you!' Canning's voice was a snarl.

The two men in the hall heard a tiny metallic tinkle. Spratt's fingers found the door knob. He whispered, 'Now!' and flung the door open. For a second or two bright light hampered them. Then their visions adjusted.

Canning was standing in front of the empty fireplace. One of his great muscle-swollen arms was holding Gaye Henson, white-faced and shaking, in front of him. In the other hand he held the Walther automatic. The barrel, covering Pelford, who stood rigid halfway across the room, shifted slightly, to menace the newcomers. The thought flashed across Spratt's brain that this was not a man to be taken by surprise.

Pelford whirled to face the policemen, then froze again at Canning's barked order. There was a moment of complete immobility, a film stopped in mid-track. Spratt's voice broke it. He spoke pleasantly, almost amusedly.

'Hullo, what's all this then? We found the front door open — '

'Shut your trap, copper!' Canning grated. 'I'm leaving — in a hurry — and you aren't going to stop me.' He gave the girl he held a push forward, towards a small table where a leather-tabbed ring lay with its attached keys.

'Go on, pick them up. Put them in my left-hand jacket pocket. Move yourself, now!'

As Gaye Henson obeyed, Dykes, matching Spratt's tone, said, 'We didn't come here alone, you know. We have men all round the house.'

'That so? Then you can feel damned sorry for any of 'em that get in my way.' The automatic lifted slightly. 'The keys, Gaye!'

She picked them up, her fingers trembling as she slid them into Canning's pocket. Dykes spoke again.

'You seem to be in a very desperate mood, my friend. Which suggests you've done a very desperate deed. Whatever it was, you won't help yourself like this!'

Canning didn't reply. Still holding the girl firmly and with his gun steady, threatening the policemen, he began to back towards a door in the far corner of the room.

We could rush him, Spratt thought — or could we? Somebody would get hurt, and it would likely be the girl. At his side, Dykes had gone tense and Spratt could read his brain as if there had been a teleprompter fixed to the opposite wall. Dykes was hating the idea of letting a man get away from him, he was struggling against the urge to lunge forward, yet there was, there must be, the restraining thought that a posthumous medal and a pitifully-scanty pension for his widow was a game not worth the candle.

Canning, near the door now, suddenly heaved Gaye Henson bodily up with his left arm and flung her forward. She screamed, crashing into a chair and falling helplessly with it. Canning turned, jerked the door open, slammed it shut behind him. They heard his feet thudding away along a passage. Dykes leapt the prostrate girl like a hurdler and went after him.

Spratt turned and ran back across the hall, out on to the steps. He filled his lungs. 'Dick!'

'Here, sir,' Garrett's voice came from the darkness.

'Canning's loose with that gun! He's making for the garage. For Pete's sake, don't try to stop him. We'll get him later!' But in spite of his own words, he hurried along the terrace towards the garage, and Garrett moved as fast as he could in front of him.

Dykes, lost in a maze of unfamiliar passages, was blundering in the direction of the kitchen. The slam of a car door, the roar of a powerful engine, hit his ears and those of Garrett and Spratt as they converged on the garage. A beam of light shot out of the stone archway, steady at first, then suddenly jerking, weaving. The car, gunned into fast acceleration, flashed through the archway, swung towards the drive with its open gates. The Deniston men had a glimpse of Canning, sawing desperately at the wheel. Suddenly, the Saab was in a wobble, then an uncontrollable spin. It left the drive, crashed into a stone pedestal urn, cannoned off it, across the grass to hit the bole of a tree, head on and at speed. The night was hideous with the smashing of glass, the crunching of metal . . .

Canning was slewed round in his seat when they reached him. He was moaning faintly, half-stunned from the crash of his head against a window pillar. Spratt reached in and picked up the Walther from the seat beside him. He turned as Dykes came running.

'It's all right — he's harmless. You can take him.'

Dykes flashed a torch along the car. 'Both wheels flat. No wonder he crashed. But you'd hardly expect — '

'I let the air out of them, Mr. Dykes. I thought it was a good idea. I happened to be up here again this evening, I was listening outside the window, I slipped round the other side of the house — '

The torch jerked round, to show Colin Taylor coming towards them. Garrett laughed shortly.

'I might have guessed it!' he said.

20

'And that just about wrapped it up,' Spratt told Chief Superintendent Bill Hallam sixteen hours later, in Hallam's office at Regional H.Q. in Deniston. 'Dykes rounded up Tenby and the Graham woman, and we had a real choir with everybody, including Pelford and Miss Henson, singing their hearts out. Molly Bilton was there, too. She'd merely changed Whitsea hotels, for personal safety reasons. She thought Canning might be after her, too, you see.'

'I don't see,' Hallam complained. 'At least, not yet.'

'Oh, Tenby knew where she'd gone. He rang to tell her we'd got Read. Molly's loyal — you have to give her that — she breezed in to Whitsea Central to do what she could for the Read family. The Kendalls were still missing when I left, but they'll be picked up before long.'

Hallam looked at the notes he had

made while Spratt had talked.

'Let's see if I have the whole picture, Jack. Pelford saw the prospect of some good pickings in Whitsea so he took this off-beat hotel as a cover. He was responsible for the hotel and store robberies we were called in to deal with. He and Canning, with Mrs. Graham as accomplice, cleared out the Palladium box-office after Mrs. Graham had telephoned him that the doorman had been sent home that night.'

'Her yarn that armed men did it being entirely false, sir.'

'Quite. And Tenby, the snout, was working for Pelford, tipping him off wherever there was a good job to do. Then Molly Bilton and her crowd moved in, also out for what they could get.'

'Yes, sir. Molly was aiming at one job, the town's biggest jeweller's. Tenby was her contact man there, too. How she got in touch with him originally we haven't yet discovered.'

'And Molly needed a peterman for that job, so she brought Lever along, plus the Kendalls and the Reads. The boy, Colin

Taylor, was right when he said Lever wasn't dropped outside the site but was taken in, concealed in the van. Lever was a man of violent temper and a Casanova to boot. So he made a big pass at Mrs. Kendall there in the caravan, Kendall came in on the big scene, swung at Lever, who pulled out his gun and squeezed off. Then when Kendall went down, Lever panicked and scarpered, dropping the gun.

'Which Read picked up and pocketed, afterwards going on to the cliffs and loosing off at a couple found there, deliberately missing. His object being to make everyone think the site gunman was still at large. All clear so far.' Hallam turned a page.

'Read was in the town with Molly when they saw Colin and Garrett, with Dykes. Molly made Colin's acquaintance and heard his story of the man he'd seen at Healthways and who he was sure was the gunman.'

'He was right, of course,' Spratt put in. 'Lever knew Pelford was in Whitsea, he'd worked with him before and it's possible

Pelford had been in touch with him, though we can't prove that. Anyway, Lever went to ground at Healthways, and Gaye Henson put us off by describing the man she said had paid a visit that Sunday morning in such a way that, while her description couldn't be seriously challenged by the gardener, Bailey, it didn't seem to fit the Kendalls' description of Lever.'

Hallam consulted his notes again. 'Molly tried to bargain with Pelford — yes — 'some indiscreet words' — I quote her — tape-recorded. Read was sent to investigate, Colin followed, got caught. Garrett was put on to Tenby.'

'With Canning — though we didn't know this at the time, sir — witnessing the meeting of Tenby and Molly. So Puffer had to be straightened up properly. Hence the conference at the fish pier, with Read, also on the sleuth, breaking it up with a couple more shots. The Bilton lot wanted to prise Puffer away from the Pelford crowd.'

'And meanwhile,' Hallam commented, 'Dykes had Lever's corpse on his hands.'

'Because Lever had been up to his old games at Healthways, with Gaye Henson, whom Canning considered as his personal property. Canning probably didn't mean to kill Lever, he just held on to his throat that second too long. Then he had to dispose of the body. Bad luck for him that Read was still on the premises and saw him putting Lever into Pelford's Saab.'

'A fact which Molly used as a means of getting that tape recording safely into her possession.' Hallam nodded. 'But Canning didn't feel happy while Read was still around, so he planned to get him, too. Pelford wouldn't have that, hence the scene at Healthways when you got there last night.'

He flung his pencil down. 'Lord knows how they'll all be charged, Jack, but that's not our concern. You've done the job you went to Whitsea to do, clearing up the robberies. So, as far as we're concerned, the box is shut.'

'And, meanwhile, sir, I have a few days' leave due. I'd like to take it now.'

'Of course, Jack. Any plans?'

'Yes, sir. I just feel like a few days at the seaside. D'you know, I think I'd enjoy them.'

THE END

We do hope that you have enjoyed reading this large print book.

Did you know that all of our titles are available for purchase?

We publish a wide range of high quality large print books including:
Romances, Mysteries, Classics
General Fiction
Non Fiction and Westerns

Special interest titles available in large print are:
The Little Oxford Dictionary
Music Book, Song Book
Hymn Book, Service Book

Also available from us courtesy of Oxford University Press:
Young Readers' Dictionary
(large print edition)
Young Readers' Thesaurus
(large print edition)

For further information or a free brochure, please contact us at:
Ulverscroft Large Print Books Ltd.,
The Green, Bradgate Road, Anstey,
Leicester, LE7 7FU, England.
Tel: (00 44) **0116 236 4325**
Fax: (00 44) **0116 234 0205**

THE MAN WHO WAS NOT

John Russell Fearn

Gerald Dawson was the first to die — in an apparent road accident. But when members of his family receive telephone calls informing them of their own imminent demise, and the predictions come true, it's evidently the work of a serial killer. Police at Scotland Yard call in Sawley Garson, a specialist in scientific puzzles. Garson will need all his skills if he is to save the remaining Dawsons from the killer — a man who appears not to exist.

THE GIRL CHASE

Douglas Enefer

Whilst Dale Shand is on a 'private business' trip in Los Angeles, he witnesses a gun killing. Shand soon becomes caught up in a series of adventures, which sweep through Old Mexico to New York — with torrid sequences in Arizona, Nevada and Chicago along the way ... He encounters gorgeous girls, sinister men, and the eccentric and indestructible Ma McGarritty. For the first time in his career Shand finds himself both the hunter, and the hunted.

VICTIMS OF CIRCUMSTANCE

Peter Conway

During the worst 'flu epidemic for fifty years, a student nurse is found dead in her room. But Golding, the forensic pathologist, believes that this wasn't as a consequence of the virulent infection . . . Under suspicion are the senior physician, revered by some and hated by others; the pathologist, from whose laboratory the poison had come; and the registrar, who gave the fatal injection . . . There is another murder before Inspector Newton tracks down the killer — and faces death in terrifying circumstances himself.

CRADLE SNATCH

Peter Conway

Mr. Justice Craythorne is convinced that Janice Beaton is a wicked woman and sentences her to three years in prison — but later he is to discover just how wicked she is. After kidnapping the judge's baby grandson, she proceeds to terrorise his family . . . Cathy Weston leads the investigation but finds herself becoming emotionally involved with the baby's father. The physical and psychological pressures mount, and the young and vulnerable police inspector now finds herself targeted by Beaton and her sinister accomplice.